NIGHT ≋
WITHOUT
DAY ≋

RAPHAËLE  BILLETDOUX

NIGHT WITHOUT DAY

TRANSLATED FROM
THE FRENCH BY
DEREK MAHON

VIKING

VIKING
Viking Penguin Inc., 40 West 23rd Street,
New York, New York 10010, U.S.A.
Penguin Books Ltd, 27 Wrights Lane, London W8 5TZ
(Publishing & Editorial) and Harmondsworth,
Middlesex, England (Distribution & Warehouse)
Penguin Books Australia Ltd, Ringwood,
Victoria, Australia
Penguin Books Canada Limited, 2801 John Street,
Markham, Ontario, Canada L3R 1B4
Penguin Books (N.Z.) Ltd, 182–190 Wairau Road,
Auckland 10, New Zealand

First published in 1987 by Viking Penguin Inc.
Published simultaneously in Canada

Originally published in French as *Mes Nuits Sont Plus Belles Que Vos Jours*
by Éditions Grasset. © 1985, Éditions Grasset et Pasquelle.

LIBRARY OF CONGRESS CATALOGING IN PUBLICATION DATA
Billetdoux, Raphaële, 1951–
Night without day.
Translation of: Mes nuits sont plus belles que vos
jours.
I. Title.
PQ2662.I465M4713   1987   843'.914   87-40030
ISBN 0-670-81301-X

Printed in the United States of America
Set in Bodoni Book
Designed by Beth Tondreau

The author gratefully acknowledges the support and friendship of Sydney Picasso regarding this edition.

To my father

Come lower, speak lower . . . The dark is not so dark . . .

—Paul Valéry, *La Jeune Parque*

NIGHT WITHOUT DAY

I

The problem now was how to turn away from the wide laceration of sky, deep and venomous, that blazed like a brazier over Paris. The most violent earthly landscapes, the most amazing animals, were engraved there, as if photographically reproduced, in a purple of dying angels of which nothing now shone but the refracted gold of trumpets. Under this last living light, people, birds and cars were seized with frenzy. The encroaching shadows and the general agitation gave only an illusion of wind; the heat remained. Exhausted children tripped and cried; dogs ran in circles and raised their heads to look men in the eyes. It had been a long day and now it was over. It was that holy hour when the unloved suffer most intensely. Men and girls passed one another without a glance.

≈≈≈≈≈

Alone on his seat, he had forgotten that he was wearing white, and was unaware that this white on his big lazy body could, in the general agony of the light, pierce others with a quick pain as sharp as that he himself experienced each time his gaze returned to the celestial spectacle on the horizon. He felt vulnerable, as if immersed in water, yet let himself be engulfed, offering no resistance to the noise and movement, the flashes of color, and the women's bodies that surged around him. He felt a great silence within. And he sprawled there, legs apart, inflamed eyes lost in an emptiness which stretched from the café table where he sat to the farthest point of land, which he felt he could just make out, where the last rock of France dissolves in glistening particles of air . . .

A yawning fit seized him, and he tried to control it, hoping, each time he opened his mouth, that he might vomit up the contents of his soul—a soul in which he could feel the constant motion of all of the valves and fine membranes of his own life.

A dry click roused him from his reverie: a gold lighter had fallen at his feet. He looked up and met the eyes of a full-figured young woman seated at the next table biting her lips. The word *girl* sprang into his mind, followed immediately by *blood*. Her lips must be black. All of which seemed of a piece with the twilight. He bent down and picked up the lighter.

"Another drink?" he asked, to his own surprise.

He handed her the lighter. She took it in a refined manner and smiled as if to excuse herself. She lit the cigarette she was holding and set down the lighter. All he could see of her now was her long hair.

"Excuse me," he said. "I asked you a question but I didn't hear your reply."

The long hair swung and two eyes studied him. Often, with an animal, you see two ears, a tail, the movement of the body as a whole; but so long as you haven't seen the two naked eyes amid the fur, you can't really say you've encountered someone. He didn't know how long she had held him skewered with her deep, cool, candid gaze when, abruptly, she released him.

"Certainly not," she replied quite simply.

≈≈≈≈≈

From his chair he could make out, far away, the little red cloud he had chosen among those in the surrounding blue. He might have been content; but he couldn't rid himself of the sound of her voice which went on echoing in his head. He drew no

3 ≈≈≈≈≈

conclusions, neither "I am unwell," nor "I am depressed," nor "The poor girl is shy," nor "It takes all kinds . . ." Knowing the familiar scene, he hardly needed to look around: the lovers at a distant table, hand in hand, totally absorbed; beyond them the proprietress, her yapping voice, her transparent blouse; over there the dyed blonde fiddling with her ring finger; in a far corner of the bar the character who, always using the same grubby notebook, scribbled furiously wherever there was a blank space, his forefinger bent double on a ballpoint pen: "Sex is nothing, sex means nothing. . ." Then, on all sides, bawling loudly in the hot air of July, children on their little legs; old women, shadowy in the evening light, hesitating at the roadside; and, wandering down the street, those angular, makeshift types who describe themselves with a sinister air as "the young" . . . He had only to close his eyes to see thousands thronging airport departure gates as if on Judgment Day; men and women on beaches plaintively collecting bags, towels and shovels at this difficult hour when it's too early for dinner and one must resolve to struggle onward; others in houses, apartments, on farms, hot, envious, needy; and everywhere roads, bridges, countryside, water, leaves and insects . . . There now. Summer, a cut-price splendor for all in its shining glory, the subtle humiliation of imperfection. What could this innocent beside him know of the true

≈≈≈ 4

meaning of summer? What it meant to men whose mothers had died, or (for here came one on the pavement) to the overweight with their soft gestures, or simply to an artist for whom the sun signified death? One should think, be a little attentive . . . If you happened to sit there, and sit long enough to be noticed, one ant among many; if you appeared in public at this unearthly hour; if you so evidently considered yourself an intelligent person; and, above all, if you had such a soft and private face it should be in panties, then you should not lightly reply, as she had done, "Certainly not," without taking into account the influence of summer on the general difficulty of living, starting with that of your neighbor . . .

I I

He crossed and recrossed his legs. An orange glow persisted in the trench of sky, but the rest had turned ultramarine. Nothing was right now. Somewhere faint music died. His heart ached, he didn't know why: it came from far away, or perhaps it was right there, something had happened . . . The tired air of the boulevard, the rustle of leaves, the symphony of forks, the scent of hot snails, the baffling suddenness of evening precipitated by people of mature years getting together . . . And then, rising and echoing in the depths of time, a torrent of bathwater while, weak and brave, he listens to the implacable footsteps of the woman with bleached hands who will drag him from his hiding place, strip him, and drown his last hope of happiness . . . Eh, what do I hear? Can a boy so loved by his mother cry so hard? A man waits patiently on the steps. Stark naked behind the half-open door, the guilty woman showers herself vigorously with talcum powder. She will be mysteriously back in her own bed when the boy becomes aware of the little flies, the bees and butterflies, all winged and glad, as they buzz in his room in the morning . . .

But that was thirty years ago.

≋≋≋

Without thinking, he looked again at the girl. She sat there, her lighter before her, with an air of being somewhere else. Instinctively he knew that this girl was the source of the private misery which had come over him like a chill. She was the kind of girl who, gorged with blood, makes the summer her own special privilege, an entirely personal achievement, an homage due to herself alone. She was a girl to take pride in cold water, the redness of red fruit, the desire in a man's eye, a girl (and here he clenched his fists with anger) who would carry off everything open and available in the world, an exasperating girl, one who would make a jewel of a wasp on her skin, who would return an interminable, complacent, throaty chuckle to the sycophantic echo of night, who would put to shame the warblers, blackbirds and thrushes, all the operatic sopranos

≋≋ 8

of the dawn chorus, and my God how the lungs would sing out for attention in a voice of which she was only the caretaker! There she is, in the face of death, a girl to intimidate you, a little boy in pajamas, by coming to kiss you good night in a cloud of perfume, a girl to go out in the moonlight while the maid cooks noodles; there she is in all her youth, a girl to aggravate the misery of having been born, to make you run with your eyes shut tight to the end of the garden and there, there . . . Before he realized what he was doing, he had grabbed the lighter and flung it on the ground.

Then, serenely, he looked elsewhere.

"Congratulations!" he heard her say. "This time you really interest me," the young woman continued gaily, picking up the lighter.

Though a little bored with what he could see, where nothing of interest now met his gaze, he didn't turn his head.

Silence fell, their own silence, created by them, the first thing they had in common, making a little precise hole in the uproar. She could make out only his neck and the ridge of an ear. His chin on his chest, surveying his own frame, he debated with himself as to whether or not all this white he was wearing took up too much space in the dusk.

"I wouldn't mind a drink after all," she murmured.

Her voice seemed to come from a great distance.

He felt ovecome with boredom, an unexpected, immeasurable boredom. Who was this woman asking for a drink? He remembered nothing; he felt fine . . . But it was no good, he would have to speak and get himself into difficulties, to say me, I this, I that; and you? He didn't want to be bothered.

"It's dinnertime now," he said between his teeth.

"Sorry?"

"I said it's dinnertime," he repeated, his voice shaking with anger. "They won't *give* you another drink."

"Won't they? That'll be the first time . . ."

"Listen," he said, "I'm sorry, I don't run the place. Just look around you."

"Well yes, I'm looking and I—"

"Well yes, you're looking and you don't notice a thing," he nearly yelled. "Can't you see that the shift has changed? It's the *evening* waiters now!"

"Why should *that* bother us?" she exclaimed.

He gave up and fell silent. Disconcerted by this, she said nothing further. Nevertheless, his wicker chair creaking as he moved, he knew it wouldn't be long before she spoke again.

"Well, if we have to eat," she said flatly, "we don't have to eat a lot . . ."

He leapt to his feet and, his face upturned, began to pat his pockets.

. . . With nothing else to look at but the bulk of his shoulders, a veritable cliff rising above her which left her no alternative but to admit defeat, she hesitated, surprised, between his charm and his rudeness, and watched closely the movements of his thick-veined forearms, which were confined by that white cotton which smelled of sunlight; of his two hands that seemed like eight, so fast did they move; of his chest, of his thighs. She wanted to help him in some way, but the dull thudding of his hands on his body concentrated her mind on his oddity, which seemed embodied in the disordered billow of his vast shirt. More than his hands, more than his arms, more than the harshness of his voice, more than his fallen-angel air which was generally so seductive, more than anything else he might have said or done with the aim of pleasing her, a little hollow in the small of his back (because it was shown to her involuntarily; because it reminded her of the rump bone you tap to herd cows; because, swathed in white jeans, he suggested the walking wounded), for all kinds of confused and unexpected reasons that little hollow was going to win her over above all else, when all at once he turned back to her with a demented air.

"Have you seen my tobacco?" he asked.

"Your tobacco?" she cried, as if in a dream. "Where is it?"

"That's what I'm asking *you*," he said severely.

For as long as it took to pull herself together, she considered the absurdity of the situation.

"What tobacco?" she demanded furiously. "And what has your tobacco to do with me?"

"No more than your lighter had to do with *me*," he replied. "Do you think of nobody but yourself?"

"No," she said; "and you might be well advised to do the same." She turned away. "Waiter!"

"Do you wish to dine?" asked the waiter.

"No, I want to calm down!" she replied, beside herself.

Suddenly she looked at him.

"Are you an evening waiter?" she asked.

"Morning usually . . . breakfast," he said mischievously.

"She's a fighter," thought Lucas from the sidelines.

"But you're an evening waiter too?" she repeated gravely.

"Yes indeed, madame, I do both," laughed the waiter, straightening his back, only to hunch it again when someone bumped into him.

"Monsieur," said Lucas, his nostrils quivering, "we would very much like to have dinner. Will that be all right?"

"Of course," said the waiter; "come inside!"

Face to face at the restaurant table, they explored what was now their common language, the kind of language two can weave, an innocent and unique sound in the world. They talked as they had begun, with no sense of strangeness; yet, beneath the surface, they felt a vague sorrow moving within them like a strange life struggling to clutch their own. They spoke to each other without being able to share their thoughts. They hardly noticed, in their close attention to words, that they were suffocating. They exhaled a little more air than they had in their lungs, and their sighs came out as if in a different breath. Strange draughts, of unknown origin, flowed around their speech. Their tone and demeanor suggested humility. Like two old people in the snow,

fearful that their last syllables will be silently obliterated by an avalanche, they weighed every word.

Over the wine and the spray of flowers they studied each other, each observing how the other's eyes
rose and fell. Forks in hand, they opened and closed
their mouths. To some they were table number
seven; to others, more prosaically, a man and a
woman dining together. But two glowing worlds
faced each other in the lamplight.

He learned that her name was Blanche, that at
the end of August she would be going to stay with
friends in the South, that she loved her mother, and
that she had a sister more delicate than herself.

She learned that his name was Lucas, that he
hated holidays, and that he had been working for
two years on a dissertation about language and de-
ception. She raised her eyebrows and made an "oh"
with her lips. He was grateful to her that she didn't
press him on the subject. Later, perhaps, he would
tell himself he had started to love her at the precise
moment she *didn't* say, "How interesting!"

They wished to learn nothing further about each
other. All of that was of no importance, any more
than the night they knew they would finish together.

What mattered was this sorrow that stifled them,
preoccupying each individually. It gave them a
cautious, autumnal air. It was as if they had left
their flat in disorder and would very soon have to
put papers away, throw out old clothes, perhaps

shut a banging window . . . Their minds were not at rest, they would greatly have liked to be free to go home.

At the same time they amused themselves by secretly calling to mind the sort of silly, inconsequential dreams one clings to in broken sleep as to revelations of the first importance. These fortuitous images, crying out for expression, added greatly to their melancholy. The images were fugitive and meaningless, often of a domestic or material nature, often colored by irrational guilt. Suddenly, for example, the memory of a bruised pear. This might have dated from that morning, from the previous week, or from twenty years before; it didn't much matter if it still belonged in this world or not, the pear appeared there between them smelling of alcohol, its pips and stem shriveled, demanding anew to be eaten or thrown away. It was as trivial and idiotic as that; yet in a deep sense, though two parts rotten, it remained one part eternal. Each of these absurd images resembled a pinprick in sleeping flesh. They were dazed, disquieted, unnerved by them. They felt they had been touched for a second by something vital, a kind of warning or call to order. But to attend simultaneously to the voice inside and the voice outside was impossible and a faintly apologetic smile would slip into their polite conversation. Confused and abashed like two children being scolded, they held each other with their eyes, balancing there lightly. Each of them had still so much to wind up and bring to a close before they could become intimate. Neither was ready; neither could break through the triviality of the words and glances that circumstance obliged them to contribute to the fiasco.

History passed in minutes, tiny and obscure. They ate in order to live, having realized that the time left to them on this earth was infinitely greater than they had imagined. The limits were once again extended. As if at news too long postponed, they felt only despondency . . . Leaning into the lamplight like two scientists working from the same data, they were puzzled by this error of calculation which overturned their first deductions and the plans they had confidently drawn up for the future. Their observation of each other precluded the offense of a communication; they raised their eyes and felt themselves electrified by the same charge. And suddenly, as if they had incurred, by their association, a precognition of the innumerable little incidents which go to make up life, which they must now relive like two beginners, the desire took hold of them to go to bed together right away.

≈≈≈≈≈

The headwaiter was suddenly beside them, handing Blanche the dessert menu. She took it and Lucas did likewise. Understanding nothing of what they read, they handed back their menus simultaneously.

"Coffee?" said Lucas.

"Yes please."

He tried not to meet her eyes too often, for it suddenly seemed, and this confused him, that hers met in one single eye at the bridge of the nose, around which the rest of the face crumpled like cloth. Blanche had the same problem and preferred to speak with her eyes lowered, so that they hardly looked at each other for quite some time. But they looked at each other in another way, by looking everywhere else in a perfunctory fashion while making a covert tour of inspection and studying each other in detail. Calmly she noted the shape of his fingers, the triangle of hair in the opening of his shirt. He noted the pale undersides of her arms, the presence of a pendant . . . Their eyes came and went with a beating of lashes, glancing here and there and drawing no conclusions—tacitly granting themselves, while talking of other things, permission to alight wherever they chose.

These covert glances gave them a furtive air which they knew to be contrary to all the rules of behavior; but they excused themselves with the easy impunity of two strangers who retain the option of returning each other to oblivion. They saw themselves as children once more, when you were told, "Look at me when I'm speaking to you"; but they continued obstinately as they were, feeling strange excitement arise. Their fugitive glances, which avoided all eye contact, had, like caresses, opened and quickened on their naked skin and under their clothes dozens of other, blind eyes, mobile though without pupils, revolving backward and forward in the darkness, calling mournfully for the strength to see and be seen. And there lay the pity of it. Blanche had two such eyes at the tips of her breasts which made her want to open her arms, puff out her chest and cry. They each had them in the hollows of their shoulders, in the folds of their arms, at the tips of their fingers and, between their legs, a single one which wept. Their bodies echoed with a constrained lament, inaudible but excruciating, more forlorn than the cry of a cock in a sleeping countryside.

Worrying with their forefingers at crumbs of bread on the tablecloth, both watched with mystical attention the progression of that metamorphosis where everything throbs with independent life and hopes to grow wings and soar.

Serious and shy, they shrank from a familiar unhappiness. Perched on the edge of their seats, balanced on their elbows, their faces were so close that each could feel the warmth of the other's forehead.

They tried to give a little more of themselves, but

their voices, gone dry, failed them and yielded up only minimal sound; so they fell silent and, awaiting the bill, wandered in the barren desert which lay between them, where it was forbidden to cry out, to weep or rejoice.

I V

Finally they rose and, relinquishing to the world at large their glasses, napkins and seats, they passed through noise, people and lights as if returning from a journey. While Blanche tugged at her skirt, Lucas raised his hands to open the glass doors; but the doors were nonexistent and they found themselves on the dark pavement, where the air was the same as inside.

She turned around, raising a hand to her hair, and lifted it with a distracted air; but Lucas, head down, his step tranquil, began to walk. She adopted the pace of someone out for a stroll who yields nothing of her independence and, putting lightness into her step and the carriage of her head lest it be thought she was following him, she followed him.

She alone knew that the keeping-her-distance, going-home-now walk she had assumed was taking her nowhere . . . Beside Lucas, who walked like a man in a dream, she heard herself walk like a woman with no objective, erratically, awkwardly, veering now right, now left, so that, pulled off course by the void of her empty spirit, she nearly stumbled at every other step. With all her power she searched among the remains of unhappy thoughts for a thought to equal in weight that which Lucas seemed to pursue along the streets and boulevards. But although she appeared normal, she had fewer memories than a drowned person. And since he said nothing further to her, since he might well think it was *she* who was saying nothing further to *him* (for both had fallen silent at the same moment); since she found it a bit much to have to do everything herself, essentially tagging along without asking questions when he was perhaps rudely heading for home; since she was unable for the moment to say what it was she wanted when in fact she wanted nothing, neither that he take her in his arms without warning at the door of his apartment block, nor that he leave her before she had grasped the significance of the evening, nor that he say a word that might spoil things or pin down something she didn't particularly want pinned down; and since at the same time she encountered here and there the odors of sex, sugar and slime, in the clear evening, in the fresh air, among the friendly people, she discovered that nothing suited her better than this haphazard, silent progress through the streets. And, in a burst of gratitude, she was on the verge of slipping her arm into his when they suddenly seemed surrounded by a crowd of overdressed middle-aged women out for the evening . . .

≋≋≋≋

With the return of summer, Paris quivered in the darkness with the same secret vigilance that clings to the edges of the great traveling circuses. A phantom fun fair had released in the city all sorts of sluggish, whispering creatures, afloat in cotton, who met and touched with the air of escaped performers; but now its clamor came from farther off. A few fire trucks passed in the light of the moon and the streetlamps. A shadowy lion stood at the corner of a bridge in the flow of life, luggage, heat and youth . . .

Meanwhile Lucas, frowning intently, hands in pockets, strode along the pavement at some secret tempo of his own . . . What physical accord could one expect from a woman whose steps, from the outset, are uncoordinated, from a woman with no idea of rhythm, not even, so hopeless was she, the rudimentary instinct of following your own, it's not difficult however (he walked faster and faster), not worth the trouble of laying her to find out, she was yet another of these liberated ones who let you do what you like, soon they would be doing it by themselves . . . He tried to stop himself, but too late; the movement of an implacable little clock carried him back and, from the beds where he thought he had safely left them, they rose up one by one . . . The ones who "know what men want," who know exactly what to do and what not to do, it's a kind of rape, you want to protest but they take you in their hands with precise, relentless gestures, it's unbearable . . . The ones who fall back to reveal white bellies, give themselves baby-fashion among the pillows and are surprised when you fall asleep on top of them before you've finished . . . The ones you hardly touch, who lose themselves in the clouds where you can't follow them, and above all don't move or you'll disturb them, there's no expectation, no hope of success, all is won and lost at the same moment, you might as well not be there, a breath of wind would have done as well, it's humiliating but they thank you afterward . . . The ones who take without giving, who demand and prescribe, who shout and insult you, their eyes shut tight, endlessly tossing and turning in the dark in search of the best position, thumping your back as if you were a mule, you force yourself to do better as their impatient cries dictate, you start to stream with sweat, the skin grows raw until finally it hurts . . .

The ones who think themselves fat and hate themselves for it but, in as much as all that flesh may give pleasure to somebody, they fall in with whatever you want, they sympathize to see you in such a state, that lot, you dearly wish they would shut their eyes . . . The ones who say you're too big for them, who cry a little, drink a lot of water and engulf you in a cunt wider than the sea, saying sorry and excuse me . . . The ones who shout no, no, I tell you no, while thinking yes, yes, and tighten their thighs and leap around like fish out of water, and later you notice them sleeping with a funny little smile, they're dreaming, be careful, they're making comparisons . . .

They returned again and again, one only, unrecognizable, lying asleep in his depths. If one day *she* came into his bedroom it would be . . . She would be hair, mouths and sky, she would be for a few hours another life form risen and breathing in the dim light while his blood roared like a tide. He would have no memories, no mother, have read no magazines, have no friends, no wristwatch, and only later would he again be a man with his head on a pillow . . . How long till she comes, how much longer to wait, tell me, Emily, she said six o'clock, how long is an hour, how long, the woman remained expressionless, holding soiled linen up to the light, you have to be quiet, she said she would come when it was dark and now it is dark, perhaps I'll hear her

2 5 ≋

coming . . . He turned his head and saw that he was alone in the middle of the street.

He called, he looked around him, he turned this way and that; for a second, for two, for three, he thought it was getting light. The pain was so intense, so much exceeded what he felt himself capable of enduring, it passed the threshold where pain is generally supposed to meet with resistance.

She was nowhere to be seen. So swiftly that he hadn't noticed, she had been assumed into whatever by its nature rose toward the sky and the stars: blocks of flats, the branches of trees. She had spun the vault of heaven on its axis and disappeared.

He turned on his heel and ran.

V

≋≋≋≋≋≋≋≋≋≋≋

With the suddenly clumsy gait of a discredited actor, her shadow trailing over stone and walls, a barely recognizable Blanche plunged into the streets. She who had been at one, a few minutes before, with the heart of this same night, happy, paired off, idiotic, her arms swinging, now dashed the sweat of shame from her face. Even were she the one who had taken leave without a good-bye or a thank you, even were she the one who had somehow failed in tact or demeanor, even were she the one whom the magic of a summer evening had deceived, the fact remained that she had been treated as nonexistent since, in the time it took to adjust the straps of her sandal and look up again, her companion was already no more than a shadow pitching headlong on the horizon. And, watching him disappear, she thought: a housepainter scurrying along the edge of the earth, a dead man already . . .

≋≋≋

She walked quickly, on the verge of tears, her hair flying behind her, her short skirt climbing her thighs, watched by a man alone, wide-eyed. Go ahead, monsieur, have a good stare, the curtain is rising all right but it's tomorrow, the show, nine o'clock, the casino at Cabourg, you bastard! Tomorrow I'll be singing fit to knock you sideways, tomorrow I'll be all wired up, but this evening I ask for no one's sympathy, I don't want to be distracted, I don't want to talk any more, I don't want to be intruded upon either with words or with sex, no one human being can understand me; one, two, three hundred people listen when I sing, taking me by the hips, thrusting themselves into me right to the very throat, grabbing and scraping and tearing out my guts and whatever else of me is detachable. From this moment I want no questions, no advice, from anyone. Not even from you, Mummy. I would go so far as to say, least of all from you, Mummy; not a word. Drop it; leave me alone. Instead of the dust, the linen, the deed box, I shall wriggle free, now that I'm twenty-five, from your kisses, your love, your support, your fervor and your immense devotion, or I'm lost. That's the way it is in this life, you must no longer come running if you hear me cry, even if nobody else comes running, for you will always run faster than a man and they can tell, men hear you running, it sounds like the thunder of cavalry and it cuts the legs from under them. And in the morning I feel terrible, I have to tell them, you know my mother, she's wonderful, she's re-markable, she has never been like other mothers, she hung cardboard witches and shiny fish from our bedroom ceiling, she peeled the skin from each little bead of a grape which she placed in our mouths with the tips of her fingers, she rose at dawn to draw, in the condensation of the windows, the out-line of a family of elves who had frolicked on our roof-tiles during the night, she brought back bis-cuits and crackers with the shopping, she gave us lessons in dance and deportment, she fought with soldiers on leave in the hot summer subway who laughed at the sight of her two half-naked children, she whispered invisibly in the dark, she promised us that we would see our cats again in heaven, if they were good cats, the first time I cried she said my tears were those of an artist; now she is my manager, my accountant, my guide, my guru, you're a nice fellow, if you want to see me again give her a call, she'll arrange it . . . It's not your fault, Mummy, nor mine either, no I don't want you to die, no I don't want to leave you, there are no two ways to say good-bye, saying good-bye starts with you not concerning yourself further with my linen, it starts with you not listening to me sing anymore, it starts with no longer sedating and boosting me with the kind of encouragement only you can provide, you are the only one on this earth who believes in me, Mummy . . . Saying good-bye starts with telling the truth, that you and Daddy weren't the whole world, that what you told us about it came only from your own mind and from what you yourself fiercely wished to believe about it in order not to break down sobbing; that the world, the real world, is not very pretty and that in this world you, my first omnipotent love, can never be my husband, my wife, my nursemaid or my future; that you can never even keep the promises you made me, that what you promised me, what you let me dream and glimpse, you promised glibly since you knew that a decisive moment would come and lo, here it is . . . But of the sexual ecstasy you promised and announced: "At that moment, children, a woman leaves her body, she sees pine forests, rivers in spate, the most piercing glaciers, it's night and yet the sun is enormous," et cetera et cetera, I'll never get over it . . . You should have told us first that if we wanted to go on being kissed as sincerely, as wholeheartedly as you kissed us night and morning, we would have to look for a long time, endure a whole series of trials, with always the chance that we would never come across anyone but the kind of cripples who hid behind tree trunks in the forest, men you frightened us with when we were children, pursing your lips in silence: "And then . . . ," you would say. And then? Then what, Mummy? What happened next? Have you forgotten what happens? But now the children know what happens. They've seen it, they've learned it at a great cost. They can tell you what happens, how the fairy tale starts to terrify, how misleading your account was, and how, to ensure fifteen years of happiness for your children, you prepare them for fifty years of shock and disillusionment . . . Not like that, it wasn't supposed to be like that. I look at children now; they know it all. Maybe they aren't as happy as we were, but they will certainly be happier adults . . . Even the wolf isn't, or isn't any more, like what you said . . . It's a poor threadbare creature, overtaken by events, of whom no one is afraid now, you pass it every day on the street without even noticing it, it's done for, a shadow of its former self, men have dreamt up more frightening things, it's of no use now except to the depraved and the deprived in search of violent sensation, who gather it up, take it home for an evening, and shake it in an effort to recreate its old effect . . .

Without understanding how she had got there, she suddenly found herself outside her own apartment house. She recognized the entrance, pushed open the door with her shoulder, stepped over a vagrant in the courtyard, pressed the light button beside the dustbins, rattled the keys in her bag; and, even as she performed these familiar actions like so many proofs of her dutiful life, something told her she was doing so for the last time.

V I

~~~~~~~~~~~~~~~~

From the knife on the table, from the bodywork of
cars parked at the curb, from the ice buckets carried to and fro by the waiters, from jewelry and
wristwatches, wherever he turned his eyes, flashes
of sunlight struck him like bombs from a silent war.
Behind his sunglasses he watched the bustle of the
day. The lingering taste of the coffee he had drunk
bewitched the atmosphere, but the fierce light forced
him into the open and filled him with dismay. He
sat in the same chair as the day before. Only the
waiter's face was different. The world had slept. As
he had seen night fall, so too he had watched day
grow and his surroundings change. The resin of his
sunlit skin sedated him. Noticing his own smell he
breathed it in and loved it. Lunchtime had come

painlessly, and had brought the sea to the foot of the street. With the same hunger, on the edge of the same void, his stomach and the sky inhaled each other.

≋≋≋

It came to seem increasingly unlikely that someone who had taken shape in an evening, before fading back into the darkness, would show herself again in this strong light, in this din. Around him other people went on with their lives, while he felt himself grow old and tired. He gazed slowly around and recognized nothing. The harsh reality of twelve forty-five disclosed that the girl beside him was a man, that nothing was more forgetful of lived experience than a pavement, a table and chair. It was a waste of time to examine, trembling with excitement, the little violin bow held by Mozart at the age of eight, no atom of him survived in the wood fibers; yet the objects Blanche had seen and touched the night before still shook him. He felt like a youth wet behind the ears for having come, with such seriousness and yet such simplicity, to sit in the same chair in the belief that this would somehow make her materialize once more. He folded his sunglasses, picked up the bill and raised a hand, and at that moment she appeared behind the waiter and saw him wave.

She presented herself with a dutiful air.

"Good morning. You wished to speak to me?"

He pushed his chair precipitately aside and stood up, one hand on the back of it.

"Not at all," he said.

"Do forgive me. Are you leaving?"

"Obviously."

"How fortunate. It's impossible to find a table."

She tossed her hair and turned nonchalantly toward the street. Both looked around for the waiter, listening once again to the private silence between them.

"May I ask you a question?" said Lucas.

"Of course," she laughed.

"It consists of one word: why?"

"Why what?" she replied, raising a hand to her hair.

He reached out and held her wrist.

"Cut it out, will you? Leave your hair alone. I've come back here for one reason only, to ask you a question: why?"

Suddenly she gave him a look so direct, so hard, that he blinked: never before had he met the like except in goats.

"You're not right in the head," she murmured, shaking her own in commiseration. "I'm sorry, you can ask your question as often as you like and in as many languages, why, *pourquoi, warum* . . . I tell you I haven't a clue what you're talking about."

"I'm sorry too," he said, turning away. "I thought we understood each other."

"Try putting it into *words* and see if I understand."

"I must say, you're not very quick on the uptake."

"No?" she retorted. "Frankly, your own conversation last night was so fascinating I could hardly keep my eyes open."

He took out his wallet and placed money on the table.

"I'm sorry to hear it," he said, preparing to take his leave. "I thought last night I'd been particularly eloquent. Somehow I had the notion you'd understood me."

"Really?" she said ironically. "Would it be permissible to know what on earth you were talking about?"

He remained silent, his eyes upon her; then he reached out and put his hand on her waist. Gently, he drew this strange body toward him and enclosed it in his arms. They stood motionless, listening to each other breathe as if in a light sleep. Their chests rose and fell in the shadows where they were standing, and they let their bodies begin to know each other and establish an intimate relationship; the slightest distraction would have alarmed them.

They hid their faces in each other's necks, heads bent on each other's shoulders as if in expectation of the whip. Time passed; then a whispering reached their ears. Voices rose, scandalized to the point of rage, and fell abruptly silent. Standing they didn't know where, they were no longer aware of their feet, or their heads, only of the down on their arms lifting and shivering in the sunlight. Somewhere they abandoned a hopeless fight lest what had happened between them should vanish once more in the depths, something as urgent as a life separate from their own, a third life which, morally more than physically, forbade them to separate. The burden was heavy, but they took the weight of it in their legs, they clung to each other, they concentrated harder, their clenched fingers hurting. Around them, chairs moved. They hesitated, amid the hubbub of the restaurant, between the urge to somehow consummate their secret mission immediately and the wish to vanish in a puff of smoke and never meet again. Suddenly all the customers on the terrace seemed to be on their feet at once. The clinking of change, the clearing of throats, were suddenly more distinct, and a voice nearby detached itself from the uproar:

". . . I've got work to do . . . There's a hotel across the street for that kind of thing!"

In a cacophony of broken glass, falling chairs

and cries of outrage, Blanche found the waiter at her feet, holding his jaw with one hand.

Lucas, surrounded by staff and customers, shook a fist and pointed at Blanche.

"That creep," he shouted, "insulted my wife!"

All eyes turned to her.

VII

In a little less than seven hours (two for the drive, one for rehearsal with the technicians, time to meet everyone, to put on powder and makeup) she was due to go on stage, and here she was, still in Paris. She hadn't had lunch, she still hadn't found a way to take leave of this strange young man who was gravely leading her by the arm as if beginning a hundred years of life together, evincing such complete confidence that she would need special reserves of courage to dare tell him, "I've someone to meet, I'm not free this afternoon." He made no demands, asked no questions, he had woven around them a veil of eternity where life seemed already transparent; he was leading her gently toward his lair. She watched herself go along with him, unable to act. In this elevated sphere where he had placed her, the air was so rarefied she lacked the strength to say: "Listen, I'm a singer, my public awaits me!"

"Blanche!"

They turned—Lucas first, his eyes starting out of his head.

Two girls elbowed each other and crowded around them.

"Wasn't you at the Caveau des Princes last winter?" said one.

"Yes," said Blanche, "that was me."

"See, din't I tell you?" cried the girl to her friend. "We saw you there; you was fabulous. My friend couldn't believe it was you."

"It was wild, what you did with your voice," murmured the other.

"We never thought we'd have a chance to tell you, know what I mean?" added the first, her hand on her heart. "You kind of . . . *shone*, know what I mean? Fantastic!"

"What are you doing now?" asked the other.

"Gala nights in the country," answered Blanche, smiling and avoiding Lucas's eye. "Tonight, if you want to know, I'll be at the casino in Cabourg."

"Great," said the girls. "Good luck!"

Blanche thanked them and they went off chattering.

They found themselves face to face once more. She glanced at her watch.

"What was all *that* about? You *sing*?" said Lucas, his face white.

"Yes," she replied briskly; "but if you don't mind I'll tell you about it another time because right now I am very, very late. Excuse me."

She hailed a taxi and opened the door.

"Just a minute, please!"

He took her by the arm and made her get out of the cab; but as soon as she was on the pavement he pushed her away as if he had been burnt and said nothing further. Amid the deafening noise of car engines he took out his pipe and tobacco. Over her shoulder she saw the taxi drive away. Eyes lowered, perfectly serene, he gave her a pipe-filling demonstration.

". . . So?" she yelled.

"So," he said, "why are you in such a state?"

"What a nerve!" she cried. "What—"

He interrupted her with an air of concern.

"Are you sure it isn't a matter of life and death? Because if it is . . . But you know, if the man is dead already it's too late in any case . . ."

"Fuck you."

He raised an eyebrow.

"The deceased must have been very dear to you."

She shuddered all over, she rolled her eyes, she began slowly to back away, wondering how best to escape.

He pocketed his pipe and took her by the elbow.

"Where are you going?" he said. "I'll take you there."

"Porte de Saint-Cloud."

He walked along with her.

"And then?"

"There's a car waiting for me there," she said.

"How much time have we got?"

"Ten minutes."

"You'll be there."

Head high, he guided her before him, making a way among the pedestrians, taking charge of everything. She wanted to weep. My wife. My wife. Her elbow aching from his grip, they stepped out briskly, turning to left and right. Why so fast, and where are we going? Couldn't we take a minute to embrace? . . .

He stopped under a tree. There she saw, broad and lithe, its muzzle bowed, in a magic space speckled with shadow and sunlight, a motorbike. She watched Lucas go up to it, open the padlocks and, with graceful movements, withdraw the chains. Birds sang in the tree; the shadows rippled like water. This splendid machine was being prepared for her. The skin of her arms and shoulders had become as sensitive as the first time she slept naked. She felt so warm, the love she felt for the whole world was so akin to pain, she thought she couldn't contain for another minute her need to cling to this man from behind and rush into the wind. He took two crash helmets from a saddlebag and handed her one. He kicked the bike from its stand and walked it to the road, where they exchanged the complicit glance of great departures.

She had right of way, she was on her way to sing. At that very moment men and women at the seashore remembered they had an appointment with her at the end of the day. Heads framed in car windows turned at their approach. Although she remained on the pillion purely by dint of squeezing her thighs together, she imagined herself for a moment, in the pennantlike flapping of her frock, to be a prominent national figure, a symbol of the Republic. The slight feminine scent inside the helmet didn't bother her, it was the smell of life and its trials, she inhaled it to the point of drunkenness; she would sing for this woman too.

When he slowed down behind a truck she yelled over his shoulder:

"Where were you taking me last night?"

He raised his visor.

"To the cemetery!" he shouted.

He was in excellent humor.

"My parents are there!" he shouted once more. "I wanted to show you!"

He lowered the visor and accelerated with a vigorous jerk of his wrist.

≈≈≈≈

A few minutes later, she pointed out to him a man standing at the corner of a boulevard. He drove her there and she called out from the bike:

"François!"

Astonished, the man came over. She laughed at the surprise she had caused, but was so flustered she couldn't get her crash helmet off. Lucas came to her assistance, tweaking out several hairs as he did so.

"François, Lucas," she finally said.

And, dismounting, she went over to the other side.

"Thank you," she said to Lucas; "you got me here on time."

Since he hadn't shut off the engine, removed his helmet or uttered a word, there was a moment of uncertainty. His eyes considered them from the slit in his visor.

"Well," she said uneasily, ". . . good-bye . . ."

Since there was no reply she added:

"I'll be back in town on Monday."

He nodded and roared away without a word.

VIII

All is black: even the night is not so dense. Perhaps she's there, holding her breath. Better not try to find her. The darkness was punctuated with horrible scarlet flowers; the blood beat in his ears. White stripes, miles of them, still flashed between his temples. He hardly knew where he was, for in less than twenty-four hours he had lost his mind.

A ray of light picked out a head in the darkness. Eyes and mouth were open, the mouth an immense crater in the center of the face. No sound issued from it, fine, you've made your point, how much longer are you going to keep me standing here? He was getting hungry. A cry as of no human voice, pitched at the very limit of its register, startled the light to a greater brilliance as it rose; he hadn't eyes and ears enough to take in what was happening. He saw a long, bare leg, so long, so bare that it hurt; he saw a violin held like a loved thing by the neck; he saw a shining pendant; he saw the profile he had been seeking all evening without knowing its real shapes, half-clothed, accentuating the rhythm of a secret impatience while awaiting the impossible consummation of this long, deep, astounded shriek. She raised the bow and, with a murderous gesture, laid it on the violin. Drawing it back and forth like a sword, she coaxed from her instrument cries softer than the cries of love, and so piercing that she rose on the tips of her toes . . . Her delicate balance, her single bare leg demanding attention, her way of approaching the treble below while being subdued by the instrument from above, her air of not being in this world even as she made this spectacle of herself . . . You had only to look at the men: whatever she was telling him by all this she was telling them too. He could see her as clearly, in fact, on their faces as on the platform . . . He crossed his legs and sat facing the hall.

≈≈≈

It was all dinner jackets, muslin veils, open mouths, shining eyes: a whole crowd motionless in the subdued light, seeming to breathe in and out of a single chest. Her bare leg, reflected from pupil to pupil, lit up, right to the bar, a forest of bare legs. The atmosphere was funereal, the odor sickly; the music, to which he wasn't listening, tore at his closed ears. He recognized the world of predators who run baths at midnight, who spare neither sun nor moon, who prefer champagne to thought, who wink at children; he recognized the pansy faces, the wincing *cognoscenti* who shit themselves with admiration; impatiently he recognized their way of crowding round a thing of beauty with the fastidious absorption of confectioners; and, in his need to discover exactly what she was up to, he turned his attention to the platform.

The only woman on earth whom, at the moment, he would have loved to hide from God and the rest of them, was fighting for her life there with a note purer and more attenuated than spun glass; clutching her violin, she prolonged that note till you wanted to cry. He would have given the moaning of the creature trapped in the chimneys of his childhood home, the squeak of the garden gate, all his dearest memories of sound, for that suspended note as he heard it fly, clear and free, from Blanche's lips—when suddenly, head back, throat distended, eyes shut, her violin at her side, she started whistling . . .

He had to keep reminding himself, or else he was

lost, that this woman knew him, had already spoken to him, that she already carried within her something of himself, the two syllables of his first name and perhaps, on a dress in her dressing room, a hair; but he felt weak, as if it was his own life which had flown from that mouth. He was devastated by an imperceptible cataclysm, nothing of what he thought he knew, nothing that he had learnt or experienced, supported him as much as the brocade velvet chair he was sitting on. It was a Friday evening in the July of his thirty-eighth year, he was unhappy, and there was no one in the world (no grandmother, no cousin, no barman, not even the woman he had come to see and who believed him to be still in Paris) who could say: "Lucas Boyenval, at this moment, is at such-and-such a place on earth, that's where you'll find him . . ." Among the millions of chairs in the world he had chosen this one and sat down without anyone objecting, he had gone right ahead without interruption, without anyone trying to stop him . . . Shocked by the freedom granted to him, he found himself sole custodian of his life in the semidarkness of a nightclub shaken by the Atlantic.

≋

Perhaps if he fell from his seat . . . Men would stretch him out on the floor of the casino. They would search his pockets and look at one another empty-handed, arms outspread. It would be up to her. Bent over his body, she would silence the murmurs with: "I know him. His name is Lucas. His parents are dead and he's writing a dissertation on language." And for a whole evening he had let this paragon of womanhood fiddle with a piece of bread on a table! He had been barely polite, had shown no curiosity about her, hadn't even bothered to ask if she wanted a dessert, and had led her halfway across Paris as fast as her legs could carry her when he should have been thinking of the musician's sleep, protecting her wrists and ankles! Seized with self-disgust, he imagined himself stopping the show, running toward her, shouting up at the dais, "I'm sorry, I'm sorry! I realize what I've done, I'll be different in the future, I was stupid, I thought only of myself, how can I undo what I did?"

But he was still seated, and Blanche like a sailboat in the night. There was nothing between them, really, except in his mind. Already he could hear the little "Hi, how's it going?" with which she would greet him in passing, her troubled eyes probably wondering at the same time, "Now where did I run into him before?"—while, amid backstage excitement, young bucks in T-shirts, bearded fellows naked to the waist, soaked in her music, familiar with her sex life, her habits and her future assignations, would take her by the arms and carry her off to other towns, other admirers, other triumphs . . . He recalled the casualness of her reply, "Certainly not," the naturalness with which she had responded to the two girls who recognized her in the street . . . If only she could have been more ordinary, a girl from Nîmes, a beautician; but the smiles, the motorcyclists roaring up out of nowhere, the restaurant dinners and parting embraces were, for her, all in the day's work. It hadn't been such a bad idea, after all, to start by making her walk several miles, cursing under her breath: that couldn't have happened to her very often. But this morning in the restaurant . . . ? How predictable, how boring it must have seemed to her when he stretched out his hand toward her body! A tremor went through his stomach. Thinking back on that for the hundredth time, his eyes shut for the hundredth time for fear of having exhausted the experience by constantly reliving it, he let the magic moment revive: the faint mingled scents of skin and soap, the firm touch of their bodies against each other, the shaking in the knees, the hipbones, the wind gleaming around them, the smell of daylight and grilled meat in the hair caught in their eyelashes. The tremor pierced his stomach again, it happened every time . . . He hadn't dreamt that moment, it had really happened, she couldn't deny it, there had been witnesses. His case rested upon it, he wouldn't leave it alone, he would obstinately repeat: since the moment could happen once, why not a second time?

The thought emboldened him and, with the invincibility of one who has suffered enough, he committed himself anew, willing to give her all his attention, when, at that moment, while he was no longer expecting her to sing, she began to sing . . . And when he had survived the prelude, when, having deliberately prolonged the impatience of her audience and distracted their mood, she finally flung her song at them with all the fury of a stripper casting aside her last stitch of clothing, he rose abruptly and went out.

I X

Between carpets and ceilings, through the corridors
and lounges of the casino, he walked to the entrance hall of the Grand Hotel. Twilight deepened
beyond the windows. Here and there, ladies clutching evening bags waited to go in to dinner. Shouting
and giggling, pages scurried from cars to elevators
in a cloud of powder and brine. He spoke to a man
at the reception desk.

"A room, please."

"We're full up, monsieur. All I have left is a
suite."

"I'll take it," said Lucas.

"For how many, monsieur, and how long will you
be staying?"

"I'll let you know," said Lucas, looking the man straight in the eyes and smiling.

≋≋≋

He opened the windows, threw back the bedclothes, unbuttoned his shirt and ran all the taps in the bathroom. The cries of gulls, the roar of the tide and the wild light on the horizon gave a stupefied air to his satisfaction with this orderly and luxurious sepulcher, its chairs, lampstands and dressing tables formal as a tomb. He contributed a handkerchief, newspapers, a dictionary, files, a small alarm clock; then he took off his clothes. He lit his pipe and went to stretch out in a warm bath.

≋≋≋

Unguardedly, his eyes were considering the veins in the porcelain, the huge washbasin, the plumbing arrangements, the height of the walls, the shape of the bidet, the symmetry of the black studs in the gray-tiled floor, when there appeared in the steam a red Porsche, headlights in a forest, a Buick convertible with its hood aimed at the stars. All the car doors open at once and there stands his father in a white dinner jacket, a cigar between his teeth. His mother stretches out her long legs and kicks off her shoes on the grass. Anne-Clarisse laughs continually, one shoulder strap hanging free, a flower pinned to her dress falling loose; thunder growls on the far side of the world. A tree trunk floats in the middle of the lake. Uncle Edward, sweating, undoes his bow tie, also Eric de Grandchemin, also the lawyer. An owl hoots, the clearing echoes with the knocking of beaks. From the mauve veils of her dress his mother raises her arms to the moon. I can see you, Adrienne, and the eyes of your jealous husband, the glow of his cigar. She snags a veil on a branch—look!—and comes away in a whirl that disrobes her from head to toe. Anne-Clarisse unfastens everything, her ball gown falling to her ankles. Great confusion now, drunken cries and a rustle of trousers from the cars: "Aren't you coming, René? Aren't you too hot, René?" . . . The women throw off their jewelry and fling their underwear at the sky; they hold hands, and their two great white behinds go bouncing down to the lake, while the men rush after them, protesting loudly, and dive in before them with three shattering splashes . . .

He and his father remain on the shore; she has forgotten them. He is eight years old in his little suit. Heads glide on the water, the swimmers breathe in and out in the stifling heat of the night, Eric de Grandchemin drifts on the tree trunk, the water echoes like a cathedral, wild creatures watch from the forest. His eyes on Adrienne, one hand in a pocket of his dinner jacket, his father smokes in silence. She throws out two tiny white arms in front of her, swimming away from the pines. Anne-Clarisse and Uncle Edward are at the other end. The lawyer is nowhere to be seen; but suddenly he springs up between the two white arms. She makes a muffled exclamation, not that she seems afraid. There isn't much to see, and nothing more is heard except a kind of low monotonous moan as if she's saying to him over and over, ". . . you . . . you . . . you . . . you . . ."; and once or twice they can be heard laughing. The cigar spins a red spiral down to the water, where it goes out, and the dinner jacket falls at his feet. Are you going to swim too, Daddy? But his father is already knee-high among the tree roots; his shoes stand on the shore. His long body slides under the water, and for a moment the moonlight gleams on a cuff link . . .

Down there under the pines, in a ghastly up-heaval that sucks down heads and limbs, stifles garglings and chokings, a great vitality seethes and whirls until, from the edge of the forest, the lawyer runs out shrieking, his arms in the air . . . Adrienne! René! . . . Their lank hair, their two wedding rings, their mouths choked with slime . . . Anne-Clarisse, Uncle Edward and Eric de Grandchemin dash off in every direction round the lake. The dark water is still; the owl hoots; her veils hang in shreds from the tree. The growl of lightning; his shoes, his white jacket . . .

Through the open door, through the dark bedroom window, he could see into infinity. It was night now, the hotel was silent, he must be alone on this floor. The bath water was nearly cold; his pipe had gone out. His cheek crushed against the rim, he watched with one eye, then with the other, the lights of a passing plane. He no more knew what he was going to do than what he was doing there; but he started by getting up. He put on a hotel bathrobe, switched on all the lights in the bedroom, closed the door to the sitting room and looked all about him: there was something inauspicious here. The room service card suggested asparagus and salmon. He could dial 005, he could do some work, or he could return to Paris and ring the girl from Nîmes he had met the week before. He picked up the alarm clock and saw that it was after ten. A minute later, shirt open, laces undone, trousers unbuttoned, but all a dazzling white, he was standing at the casino exit as she came down the steps. She ran to him.

"Lucas! Were you there?"

Preoccupied with a feverish attempt to button his shirtcuffs, he nevertheless inclined his head politely, his heels together.

"I beg your pardon?"

"You *were* there," she repeated happily. "Did you see me?"

"I'm afraid not, I didn't have that pleasure," he said.

"But why not? What a pity! . . . What are you doing here?"

"Me? Nothing . . . I'm just here. Are you coming?"

"What do you mean, am I coming?"

He continually rubbed his sleeves and the front of his shirt in a restless manner, seeming nonplussed for a moment.

"We'd better have some supper," he said impatiently. "It's late, and I don't know if the hotel dining room . . ."

Very deliberately, she placed her violin case on the ground and, folding her arms, looked him straight in the face.

"What's the matter?" he said. "Have you already eaten?"

She made no reply, only went on staring at him. He did the same, and soon they came to acknowledge each other. Their looks softened, they blinked gently; something at once excited and desolate had entered their faces when the mood was broken by a voice shouting for Blanche.

"Go on ahead!" she called over her shoulder. "I'll see you there!"

Quietly, as if to herself, she added: "Wherever I

go there's my mother, François whom you've met, a friend of François, the friend's wife . . . I'm sorry."

He bent down suddenly and, picking up the violin case, placed it in her hands. She stepped backward away from him.

"Where's your place?" he said, following her.

"Montparnasse . . ."

"I mean tonight."

"François has a house here."

"I wish you good night," he said gravely, even as he continued to follow her.

She turned and ran off.

"Who was that?" said her mother.

"Just a friend."

"Do we carry on or should I go back and say hello?"

"Never mind, Mummy, never mind; I've already said hello to him."

"I'm speaking of myself, dear. If by any chance I know him, I don't want to seem to be turning my back!"

"Not so loud," said François.

"Why not?" said Blanche.

"Because your friend is following us, dear," said her mother. "I've been telling you so for the past five minutes."

"*Is* he, François?"

"Yes; but he has every right to go in our direction."

"We'll see when we get to the square," said her mother.

"He's quite good-looking," laughed a young woman who hadn't spoken before.

"Don't look round any more, *please*," said Blanche.

"Maybe he just wants an autograph . . ."

"Blanche has already been very nice to him. She spoke to him for several minutes."

"Shut up, all of you," whispered Blanche. "I tell you he's a friend of mine."

"Maybe someone could take a peek now?"

"No, no; I tell you no!" hissed Blanche.

"Let's slow down and see," said the young woman excitedly; "then he'll have to overtake us."

"She's right, I'm going to light a cigarette," said her husband.

"This is awful, he's still there . . . Look, he's stopped too!"

"I'm going back there," said Blanche. "Don't stick around; carry on!"

She handed the violin to François and, at a resolute pace, strode up to Lucas on the deserted road. He waited for her, his hands in his pockets, rolling a pebble around with his toe.

"I lied to you," he said, before she could open

her mouth. "I saw you singing. I left before you'd finished because I was jealous."

"I forgive you."

"I need you."

". . . Same here, I think," she murmured.

He didn't react; perhaps he hadn't heard her. She raised her voice and repeated:

"I need you too."

"I heard you."

"We ought to talk."

"Fine."

"It's a bit late tonight, but . . ."

He looked up.

"No problem," he said. "I've taken a room at the Grand Hotel and I've some work with me. What time shall I expect you?"

"It won't be before one thirty or two in the morning; they don't close the bar until—"

"Don't worry," he interrupted her. "Not only do I have a bedroom, I've a sitting room with a little fridge full of spirits and fruit juice. Come right up: room four twenty."

She smiled, but there was no answering smile. They took three paces backward before their eyes left each other, and he was the first to turn away.

X

When he had remade the bed, emptied the bath and switched on the sitting room lamps; when he had eaten the cold supper he had ordered and sent back the tray; when finally, after so much agitation, there was nothing left to do but wait, the room began to hum with the monotonous drone of passing time.

The air was oppressive despite the open windows; each minute of night made the lamps seem more unreal and ostentatious. Ears on fire, crouched over his files at the table, he forced himself to stay awake. The later it grew, the more glaringly mistaken the assignation appeared to him, spoiled in advance by the obviousness of the place, the time and the proximity of the bed, the body clean, the little suite in order . . . He suddenly saw himself like a woman waiting among her things for a nocturnal visitor—someone who had agreed to a date only at his own insistence, who treated him as he himself treated girls, who wouldn't come until after supper, with nothing to offer him but her fatigue. How could he arrange it so she wouldn't see the bed as she came in, so he wouldn't be the one to open the door, so she wouldn't hear in the sound of the door the sound of a trap closing behind her? He stood up, knocking over his chair: that door would need to be oiled or taken off its hinges. What was needed was a place without doors, walls or beds. Disorder and chance had to be reestablished, he mustn't be ready when she arrived, or better still he mustn't be there at all. He crumpled up some pages of his dissertation and tossed them on the carpet, kicked off his shoes, rolled up his sleeves and opened the door wide. He sent the bedspread flying and, grabbing hold of the mattress, heaved it, covers and all, into the sitting room, whence he returned with two armchairs, substituting them for the bedside tables. Having turned the bedstead on its side with a cracking of old wood, he managed to stand it against the wall and cover it up with the spread; then he switched off three lamps and stood back, mopping his brow. It was no longer a bedroom, and was far from being a sitting room. The place swirled with dust; the carpet was a different color now, with four deep imprints visible in the thick pile; the box spring bedframe was still quivering to itself. He tore the canvas from it, ran into the sitting room, and dragged the mattress back through the door. He felt dizzy. All that remained was to set the bedframe back on the floor and the mattress on top of it; then he stumbled into the bathroom, threw off his shirt and dashed cold water in his face with both hands. As he emerged the telephone rang.

"A lady is asking for you at reception, monsieur. Should I . . . ?"

"Yes . . . ," he said. ". . . No; tell her I'll be down."

He started in one direction, then in another, but the number of things to be done with no time to do them meant he did none of them. Everything about him bore the signs of a veritable brainstorm. Stripped to the waist, legs apart, arms clasped behind his head, he wept like a butterfly on a pin in the middle of room 420 on the fourth floor of the Grand Hotel, Cabourg. It was two o'clock in the morning of a new day, and the girl he had met in a Paris café the day before was standing at the door. She looked at the overturned furniture, she looked at him weeping behind his arms, and she wept too. They had waited too long already; now, mouth to mouth, they kissed till their lips bruised; till, heads thrown back, they stood gasping for air, hiccuping and clutching each other by the wrists.

"My heart!" she cried.

"What?"

Their tears were mechanical, they couldn't breathe; then, all at once, it passed. They straightened up and, sniffling, stared at each other without comprehension. She placed a hand on her throat.

". . . The door," she said.

"Yes; let's close it."

They walked over to it hand in hand; then, parting laterally, they retraced their steps and, holding hands again, came together beside the mattress. They bent their knees at the same moment and, seizing whatever came to hand, one a pillow, the other a sheet, to make their bed, they curled up and fell asleep.

X I

≋≋≋≋≋≋

And because it was no longer merely a question of themselves; because something else was taking place which would oblige them to set aside their own pretensions; because they were waiting for that moment with the holy wonder of a Christmas morning; because in gardens, in monasteries, everywhere, before day broke again, men and birds were singing; because she breathed with her stomach and he no longer seemed to be breathing at all; because she felt something twitch at her side like the paw of a dreaming rabbit; because, under the sheet, they heard it raining on France and on the sea; because they were delighted, in a confused sort of way, with the enormous advance represented by their being in bed together, as compared with the millions of others still at the stage of molluscs in wet sand; because bread and coffee were already invented, clothes already woven, houses built, and they needn't lift a finger; and because the last time they woke they had removed her dress, they slept face to face without really sleeping, filled with the night to come and the approach of autumn. Motionless, hidden from the gaze of the world, watching themselves as if from above, they lay wedged together with their eyes shut like two drowsy lions, apparently uninterested, either of them, in the mass of her breast gathered up between them on the sheet. He knew from the slope of the mattress that she was well endowed; she knew from his sighs that he was overwhelmed by it. Meanwhile, assured of their singularity so long as nobody touched it, they dozed contentedly.

≋≋≋

No sound could be heard in the hotel; even the kitchens were still silent. The rain had stopped, and a swarm of gray light was seething over the two solitary figures on the floor, when he leaned on an elbow.

"Now," he said.

She threw back her head and arms and, looking away, stretched out her bulging breast to him under the sheet. But, far from laying her bare, he gathered the folds around her, drew up the sheet, rumpled it in his palms and slowly heaped it on top of her . . . With her legs exposed at the other end of the mattress but otherwise covered up to the eyes, she could see him above her fingering the linen with extreme delicacy like one of those fine cloths for wrapping cheese; and, watching him, it seemed to her that he was gazing at something other than herself when, pulling himself together, he began to remove her remaining clothes with a shaking hand.

She felt the fabric move beneath his fingers, she saw the quantity of chiffon diminish and lighten, she saw his unshaven morning face which seemed to age little by little. She kept shifting her head in an effort to see, but he set it back on the mattress. If he had been alone in a room spreading out a headscarf full of gold coins, his expression, in the oblique light, could not have been more disquieting, nor the set of his jaw more fierce. Suddenly, restraining himself no longer, he gathered up with a single grasp the last ruffles and pleats and anything else that moved.

"Close your eyes," he said.

Returning to the bundle crushed against him, he opened it with a dry gesture and looked at her breasts.

He seemed shaken, staring at their blue veins.

Evidently as excited as himself, they too were eager for what might follow. He explored them with bare hands. He had despaired of one day finding something as beautiful as these two veined breasts on a girl's body, and now he was in despair of this beauty which, his life long, he could never do more than touch, squeeze and implore. He held them in his hands like water. Disfigured by suffering, overcome with new reasons for denouncing in his dissertation the inadequacy of the verb *to possess*, he bent and kissed them. Inflamed with resolution, he raised his hips, braced his legs and, finally seized with a familiar hope and filled with a desire to make the angels smile, he parted her thighs, hoisted them on his shoulders, and entered her body.

"Blanche!" he gasped. "What are you? What are you?"

It was the first time he had used her name. Propped on his arms, he stared at her intently. Their stomachs smacked against each other; she hid her face in her hands.

"Do you want me to stop?" he went on, almost unrecognizably. "Do you want me to leave you here like this?"

He stopped on the brink . . . She withdrew her hands.

". . . No!" she cried.

"Say it, then; say it!" he commanded, starting

again. "What are you? . . . You are my . . . ?"

She lay with her mouth open. Wanted in one way, she knew nothing of any other. Her eyes searched his face.

". . . wife . . ." he murmured. "You are my wife. Say it. Say, 'I am your wife.' "

And again his urgency increased.

"I think I'm going to cry," she said.

He watched her lips open in a smile, her tears brim under his gaze, her white neck thicken; and the damage he had done overwhelmed him beyond all hope. He held her lips and closed her mouth with his, silencing her tongue in the midst of her tears and crushing her with his body. They moved fast, more and more delicately, more and more intolerantly, and, their senses subdued by the constraint of the listening walls, by the mingling of air, light and smells, by their present madness and the promise of the sea, they filled the room with a continuous whispering . . . Presently he recognized against him the barely perceptible tapping he had noticed in her legs on stage; and to feel the rhythm spread from her legs to her shoulders, to see and hear each stroke modify further the tenor of her grimaces and the resonance of her voice, made it so urgently necessary to resist a general upheaval that he was nearly unseated when she suddenly cried, "You know everything! You know everything!" and, kicking out in all directions in his arms, fighting off a thousand conflicting emotions, she abruptly burst out laughing.

Then she lost consciousness. He found himself alone, enclosed in an inert body where he dared no longer move. He raised his eyes, blinking in the sunlight which had invaded the room, and, in the sudden silence, considered the dry lips, the pale cheeks, the faint breathing—seeking, on the wall before him, the strength to await her return. But, more and more shaken by her complete self-possession, more and more excited by her interdiction, his eyes riveted to the wall, he began to probe again very gently. And very gently, very gently, she responded. He brought her back, sleepy and trembling; hot and streaming, they lost themselves in turmoil once again until, once again, she burst out laughing . . .

"You too? You too?" she begged, fainting again.

"Ah no, not me; not me," said he between his teeth.

If she let him, if she didn't talk, if she loved him as he loved himself, then this time, this time he would have his old intuition confirmed that there existed an inexhaustible woman, confirmed in the depths of this woman of whom he knew nothing, but in whose depths, for the first time in his life as a man, he would discover his goal and his fulfillment in the lonely fever of the explorer who seeks without regard to time or effort . . .

As the morning advanced, high-pitched cries rose from the beach. Doors banged in the corridor; the tinkling of cups and teapots was followed by the whine of a vacuum cleaner and the rattle of keys in locks. In room 420 the son of René and Adrienne, spreadeagled as if on a cross whose arms went from his birth to this woman and from this woman to his death, urged her on from beginning to beginning.

XII

A loud knock on the door woke him with a start, and a woman in an apron appeared in the mist and roar of the sea.

"Oh, excuse *me!*" she exclaimed, and the door closed again.

He fell back heavily beside Blanche, who shook a little, half-consciously. A strip of sunlight on the carpet struck her full in the face. He rose again at once, grappled with the shutters and closed a curtain; then he stepped over the mattress, fetched a glass of water from the bathroom and knelt to support her head.

Dried up, puffy and bruised, her lips opened with difficulty. Leaning on the mattress, he held the glass to her mouth. She seemed to be trying to say something, and he leaned closer.

"Don't . . . move," he heard her say.

He laughed aloud.

"Don't move, indeed!" he said gruffly. "You'd better drink something. Open your eyes."

She was trying to say something. He listened and watched her mouth straining to articulate.

"Don't . . . speak."

"Don't move, don't speak; anything else?" he laughed. "How about eating? 'Don't eat' either?"

He waited for a moment, feeling her breath on his hand. He blew aside the veil of hair trailing over her cheeks.

"Here, drink some water," he said.

This time her whole face shuddered, her eyelids contracted, and she seemed exasperated.

"I . . . know," she murmured.

Since his arm could no longer support her without shaking, he rested her head gently on the mattress, arranged her hair, and let her go back to sleep.

≈≈≈

Naked, hungry and happy, he went to the window, leaned on his elbows, and looked out. The recent heat had gone with the rain; the sand at the foot of the steps was still spattered with raindrops. A gust of wind filled out the awnings and rippled the flag flown to indicate that it was safe to swim here. Vast dazzling clouds, far from the sun, cast a holiday air over the whole seaside, with its flapping hats and kites. His raw consciousness, still moist and nocturnal, could hardly bear this confrontation with the infinite. After the shadowy luxuriance of the world he had just left, the openness of the sea and sky, the harshness of the light, the diffusion, the trivial cries of the ignorant little dark figures below him, the absence of mystery in the world out there, drove him hurriedly back into the room, where he closed another curtain.

Steeped in a red glow shot through with fiery lines, the disorder of the room was delightful. Moving lithely and silently on bare feet, he walked around it as if in a garden, shifting from one position to another. Hand on hip, one leg at rest, he contemplated his achievement with pleasure. All points of view converged on that silent riot of white formed at his feet by the pillows, his handkerchief, her dress, the glass of water, the underclothes of his wife, and the chaotic sheets where floated, here and there, locks of hair like a raven's wings. A little further, at the periphery of his vision, lay crumpled paper, a wastebasket, the overturned chair; then the bolster, the notecase Uncle Edward had given him when he finished his military service, the bedspread twisted like a rope; then the alarm clock, an ashtray, the telephone and suddenly, between two high-heeled shoes, a canvas bag wide open to reveal, jumbled together, a hairbrush, sandals, a makeup box, a shawl and a sheet of squared paper. He had only to reach out his hand. He read:

The necklace of pink stones from the Antilles (August '75)

The rampant lion from Lomé (Togo)

The crouching lion from Peking (1st trip)

The monkey from Garoua (Cameroon)

The little god from Abidjan

The orange dressing gown and toucan from Mexico (spring '78)

The blue cat from Murano

The two straw owls from Shanghai

The malachite rabbit (Hong Kong)

The dragon box from Peking (2nd trip)

The red ivory cameo from New Delhi (1st trip)

The scarab from Conakry

The dressing gown from Kyoto (Japan, April or May '79)

The 1st bracelet of gold beads from Taif (Saudi Arabia—lost!)

The 2nd bracelet of gold beads from Amman (Jordan)

The elephant skirt from Delhi (January '80, 1st trip)

The two glass drops and the yellow ball from Hebron (Israel)

The 1st gray slip from Sumatra

The 2nd pink skirt from Java

The fan of peacock feathers from New Delhi

The Nandi bull from Madurai

The candied fruit from Damascus.

Who would have thought, to look at her, that she had traveled so much? A chill ran through him. Even while forbidding himself a comparison with his own childhood in Auvergne, his long years in boarding school, his student years in Paris and a few enforced vacations, always in Europe, he calculated rapidly: twenty-four, twenty-five, hardly more, say fifteen years old in 1975, at fifteen in the Antilles, yes, that was possible; but at eighteen in Mexico, her first grown-up dressing gown, with Togo, China and Cameroon in between . . . A second dressing gown, only a year after the first . . . Between the first and second there had been Venice, then one, two return trips to China, India, Guinea, no, it wasn't possible . . . And then all these animals, the schoolgirl precision, the bracelet lost and immediately replaced, really it made more sense to think of these as presents, brought back perhaps by her father.

He refolded the page lovingly and, slipping it into the bag, returned to her.

≈≈≈≈≈

She had recovered some color, her face was smooth, her hair stuck to her forehead. The fine perspiration glistening on her skin seemed to glow with the warmth of contentment. He observed her eyebrows, her large mouth, the way her hands were placed; the massiveness of her sleep was somehow stonelike. Poor girl . . . Only the evening before she had sung her heart out; violently alive, she had rushed down the steps of the casino, run to her friends, and now look at her, defeated . . . How she had struggled, and how futile had been her furious assertion of her own freedom when it was already obvious that she wasn't free! Moved to tears, he held a finger to her nostrils and felt the faint breath of her life, a life which for several hours now had belonged to him, a bewitching gift come in the night all alone on her own two feet.

She moved slightly and he noticed a gold speck gleaming in a hollow of the sheet. From among the folds he drew out a tiny chain of squared links which he recognized at once as the second bracelet of gold beads from Amman . . . He closed his hand on the discovery and, deciding it was time she ate something, went to ring room service, crouching behind the bedframe and speaking in a low voice.

≈≈≈≈≈

Naked, busy and alone, he came and went in her field of vision without looking at her. This is what this man was like in the morning, and she had a confused fear of knowing it; before he could surprise her half-awake, she closed her eyes again. The logic of his gestures and motions still escaping her, she took pleasure in prolonging her childlike happiness . . . At the same time, something about being stretched out helplessly on the floor, while he was up and about, parading his health and strength before her, gave rise to a kind of fear . . .

He reappeared, dressed in a white bathrobe; then

someone knocked at the door. She watched him return with a large tray, which he placed on the table. In his zeal this morning she sensed an ardent need to make reparation for some offense as much as to show thanks . . .

She watched him tear the bread and butter it; then he turned his head and their eyes met.

They studied each other silently from a distance. Nothing in Lucas's body indicated what his next move might be. Seconds passed.

She held out her arms to him.

He dropped the knife and ran to her.

"How do you feel?" he murmured gently in her ear.

". . . And you?"

"I'm scared; I think I'm going crazy," he said quickly.

She felt his warm breath on her cheek and looked up at him.

"Didn't you sleep?"

He took her hand and stood up, about to speak.

"Hey, my bracelet!"

She put a hand to her wrist while he put his in his pocket.

"I wonder how you lost it," he remarked slily.

He smiled and dropped it on the sheet.

"It looks like a child's bracelet," he added. "Did your father give it to you?"

She gathered all her courage.

"No," she said; "my husband."

Before she had closed her mouth, he had gone to finish buttering the bread.

"Lucas!" she cried. "You're not . . . ?"

"Would you like tea or coffee?" he said.

X I I I

They ate in silence, their eyes lowered. She waited, coffeepot in hand. Even to her question, "Shall I pour you some more?" he made no answer. He kept his pat of butter for his own use, and she took another for herself. He wasn't seeing her, he wasn't hearing her. There seemed to be only one knife, which they borrowed in turn and replaced on the tray. Each sound was deafening. Blankly, she held her steaming cup to her lips, not knowing what to say next. I've deceived no one: the sentence presented itself to her mind completely formed. At the same moment, she heard herself say it aloud:

"I've deceived no one."

She raised her eyes. He hadn't reacted at all.

Severity made him even better-looking. He drank with little gulps.

"If by any chance we should see each other again," she said slowly, "your present attitude isn't very reassuring. In any case it will remain a black mark against you."

He pushed aside the tray and stretched out on his back, his hands behind his head and his eyes on the ceiling.

"If you think about it," she continued, "I owe you no explanation, though naturally there is one. It's enough, I think, that you should see how ridiculous you're being."

She stopped for a moment and asked:

"Are you listening to me?"

"I'm the one who asks the questions," he said all of a sudden.

"Just as you like."

She too stretched out, on the other side of the tray, and he began in a harsh voice:

"How many children have you?"

"We're back to formalities, are we? Okay. No children."

"How many abortions?"

"None."

"How long have you been married?"

"Seven years. But we're separated," she added. "I was fifteen when I met François."

"Ah, so it's François?"

"What?" she said, turning her eyes in his direction.

"I said, 'Ah, so it's François?' "

"That's right, it's François."

"It's even worse than I thought," he said, rising.

Picking up his clothes, he went and locked himself in the bathroom.

With a surge of energy, she scrambled to the bathroom door, hitting it with her fists and her knees. To her surprise, the door opened and he appeared, towel in hand. His face, usually so expressive, was no more than a mask. Water ran noisily in the bath. He looked down at her, where she knelt cradling her breasts in her arms, and threw her the towel.

"What do you want?"

"The bathroom, of course," she said indignantly; "for heaven's sake!"

"If that's the way you behave, no wonder your marriage didn't last," said he, moving aside. "Make yourself at home."

"If that's the way *you* behave," she replied, testing the bathwater, "no wonder you've never been married!"

And she slammed the door, which opened again at once. She drew back a few steps.

"What is it?" she asked weakly.

As he advanced upon her, she clung to the washbasin. He reached out a hand, took his things from the rack, and left without a word.

≈≈≈≈

When she opened the door again he didn't turn round. He sat at his worktable, dressed only in his white trousers. His back was broad and muscular, and his bare feet twined together as he smoked his pipe in the renewed heat, turning the pages of a large dictionary.

She slipped into the room, found her dress and panties, and put them on in silence. Then, changing her mind, she looked in her bag, took off her panties again and pulled on the bottom half of a swimsuit. She set aside her high-heeled shoes and put on sandals. Finally she brushed her hair. He hadn't moved.

"See you later," she said.

He didn't answer. Picking up her bag she walked to the door, unlocked it and went out.

≈≈≈≈

It was winter on the other side of the door. The corridor was interminable. In the electric light, between the thick walls and the soft carpet, she couldn't hear her own footsteps. Eyes hot, stomach churning, she walked in silence, no longer liking her bare arms: the strap of the canvas bag irritated her shoulder. She felt her mouth drawn down and her skin burning as if from a day in the sun. He wanted no more of that skin, he had given it back to her. She pressed a button and the elevator arrived before she had finished counting the doors with a last glance at the deserted corridor.

X I V

They can't have been very different, the feelings of those legendary creatures escaped from the water and beached on the shore of a continent. Flat on her stomach, her lashes starred with tears, she lay, oblivious to the wind, watching, in the shadow formed by her head and arms, a tiny sand flea, so nimble it eluded her each time she tried to bury it. The disconnected sound of open-air voices, the hollow thud of footballs, the rustle of a drifting newspaper, the faint barkings and cryings, came to her as if from a great distance. With the disorder of the world and the sound of the waves there mingled the exploits of the night before. When the wind abruptly ceased, when suddenly the air and its sounds stood still, each time she shut her eyes against the sting of the sun, she saw him in red flashes—remembering how, gazing fixedly at her, he had touched the tips of her breasts, straightened and rearranged her on the pillow for better leverage, taken hold of her mouth with five fingers and held it to his own like a monkey eating fruit; remembering the roughness of his chin and the smoothness of his shoulders, the hair on his thighs and the mulishness of his ideas, his style of behavior, his masculine whims . . . When she grew old, the memory of his contact with her body one summer morning (the morning he had desired her) would strike her still like an inexplicable blow. Perhaps you ran from man to man until one of them stopped you in full flight. Other men she had known, and other men she had yet to know, had moved the same way . . . But that he had had the right to open the buttons of her dress, that he had seen her naked and beseeching, that he had found her dampness and moistened his fingers there, that he had heard her cry out and weep, that he had seen her dirty, defeated and bruised, that all these images of her had entered the pupils of his eyes, and that now he could leave and take them with him, that now perhaps he felt nothing but contempt, that now he might perhaps be disgusted by the memory of her hot flushes, her sighs and her feminine arousal, all of that for the first time, through the ineluctable shame growing in her, seemed to be something she could never, in all her life, rise above or outstrip.

Her body covered with sand, her hands on her head, while there came back to her the story of those soldiers for whom time stopped during the explosion of a bomb; while there came back to her those cases of women immured forever, whom a single night of love had fulfilled for the rest of their lives; while there came back to her, in the touch of the earth, how empty she felt without him between her legs; and while, to add to her annoyance, the rise of her bottom spilt a tiny trickle of sand between her thighs, she shivered violently in the breeze, remembering his brief courtship . . . With what confidence, what determination, he had followed them to Cabourg; with what nervousness he had appeared at the casino exit; with what a murderous look he had greeted François at Saint-Cloud; how he had picked a fight for her sake on the café terrace; how, shaking from head to foot, he had taken her in his arms without daring to kiss her; in what an ungracious manner he had spoken to her at first, as if to conceal his attraction to her, then that nonsense about the lost tobacco which was no more than a pretext for showing her the curve of his thighs, as distinctly and unself-consciously as an animal . . . Through image after image, she relived the moments which had led to her own seduction

. . . Then, involuntarily recalling his phrase, "You are my wife, you are my wife, you are my wife," she knelt up and, overcome with a sudden and violent need to vomit, she braced herself on the sand.

"Can I help you, madame?" said a man's voice.

"Are you from the hotel, madame?" said another voice. "Can I fetch someone?"

Her neck bent, she shook her head. My wife, he had asked her to say she was his wife, he had announced her as such to the entire restaurant . . .

"Watch out, her hair is getting in the . . ."

Someone poured cold water on the back of her neck; someone spread earth from a child's bucket on the sand before her.

"Isn't she feeling well?" a woman called from some way off.

"She mustn't stay in the sun . . . Here, put on this hat."

She stood up.

"I'm fine, thank you, really . . . Whose hat is this? . . . Thank you . . . I think I'll go for a swim."

≈≈≈

She walked for a moment among pools and reflections before reaching the first waves. Although startled by what had just taken place, she already seemed to have left behind the person to whom it had happened. Breakers crashed at her feet; boys thrashed around her, out of breath. Knotting her hair, she waded toward the horizon. Wind whistled in her ears, sailboards skimmed the water, dangers converged from all sides. She opened her arms and swam.

She felt pretty brave, considering this was her first swim of the year. The water was heavy and cold. She thrust it aside with open fingers, and suddenly nothing seemed very serious any more. The waves rushed to meet her; chin up, she forged ahead. She climbed and descended ridges and troughs in a cloud of powdered ice, blinded by millions of glittering splinters. The sea slapped her on all sides, restoring her sensual pleasure in being alive, the infinite diversity of sensations and situations, the succession of nights and sights that constitute existence . . . Yet at the very heart of what she knew to be a significant mutation in her life, she embraced in advance the inevitability of everything in the way of conflict heaven and earth might be preparing for her, everything from the slightest happiness to the greatest suffering. But where had she got the idea that *he* had sent *her* away when, on the contrary, it was she herself who, splendidly angry, had left the room? She pictured him thrown back on himself, suffering the effects of her intransigence; and, behind the displeasure he had so vigorously evinced, she suddenly glimpsed a considerable tribute. She took a deep breath and turned back.

Among the miles of private mansions lining the coast at this point, the hotel looked ridiculously small. Its stone balconies with their canopied arches dissolved in the light; she could hardly distinguish the window on the fourth floor. Gently, rolling over on her back, she beat the water with her hands and legs; increasingly euphoric now, she felt lighter than a leaf on the surface of the sea. What with François keeping an eye on her, and Lucas, whatever he thought, awakening her to a new intensity, there were now (and how could she not laugh at the convenience of it?) two men preoccupied with her! All the more reason, then, to respect the old tie with the one while trying to contain the impetuous love of the other.

X V

She stumbled out of the water and, collecting her things, moved further up the beach, where she lay stretched out, exhausted, under the sky.

Her chastened heart still beat with the rhythm of her swim; her ears buzzed; she closed her eyes. Hands flat on the warm ground, she felt the earth beneath her slide behind the sun, and for seconds at a time, fearful of falling into the void, she clutched a fistful of sand. A childish tantrum erupted nearby, followed by the flat sound of a slap on the cheek.

"I hardly felt that!"

A short silence; then tears.

"Do you want me to slap you again? Look at my hand, Christophe! Shall I slap you again?"

Blanche raised her head; and just as she was about to lower it again she spotted Lucas, in swimming shorts, a towel over his shoulder, coming down the steps of the seawall. She lay down at once and didn't move. Blue, everything was blue. Were it not for the child's vexation, things would be nearly perfect . . .

A moment later he spread out his towel beside her and bent down to rummage in her canvas bag. She sat up.

"Why are you searching my bag?"

"I didn't want to disturb you," he said, pausing for a moment. "I'm looking for skin cream: you didn't bring it with you?"

"What cream? What are you talking about?"

"Skin cream; you know, for the sun . . ."

"I haven't any."

"What, you've no skin cream? I thought a woman always carried skin cream in her bag."

"A woman? What woman?" she said, dozing off.

"Well, my mother, for example, always had a . . ."

He realized she was shaking with laughter on the sand.

"What's the matter?" he said. "Have *you* had a touch of the sun?"

"No, I just remembered I forgot to bring your little bucket and spade too!"

She laughed wildly.

He said nothing.

Standing in the wind, wrinkling his nose, his eyes screwed up and staring at the horizon, he scratched his chest uncertainly.

"In the circumstances," he murmured, "I don't think I'll stay."

She reached out a hand and took him by the ankle.

"Come on, lie down; it's nice here."

Lucas glanced around him.

"Where am I going to lie?" he asked.

He had the same lost, submissive air she had noticed in the street the previous night, before they had agreed on an assignation. She patted the towel on her left.

"Lie down, will you? Here's your place, right here."

He dropped on one knee and stretched out on his stomach, one cheek turned in her direction.

≋≋≋

They closed their eyes. Side by side, elbow to elbow, they felt themselves complete once more. Occasionally, in the crushing heat, a long sigh escaped them. Not for a long time had either felt so safe.

"I meant to tell you . . . ," he began.

She opened one eye and looked at the ridge of his arms.

"Yes?"

"You have a crazy body . . . I've never seen anything like it."

His long puckered lashes flickered on his cheek. He spoke as if asleep, in a tired, monotonous voice, the heat of the sun dulling the rhythm of his speech.

"Your legs are endless . . . and you've hardly any stomach at all . . . Your breasts are incredibly alive . . . and your shoulders are those of an orphan . . . You've a bottom but no hips . . . Nothing goes with anything else . . ."

His lips remained open; he breathed faster, his eyebrows arched on his forehead.

". . . You're quite amazing," he concluded.

His facial muscles relaxed as he added:

"Slim and . . . full at the same time . . ."

He seemed to doze off.

She closed her eyes. A faint snoring confirmed that he was asleep. The sounds of the universe came clear again. Wind and sun pursued each other between their shoulderblades; snatches of music carried to them on the breeze. The raw smell of the tide clung to the warm skin of their arms.

"I couldn't put up with an ordinary girl anymore," he suddenly said.

"Now you're talking nonsense," she chided. "There's no such thing as an ordinary girl; everyone is extraordinary."

But at the same time, lest this annoy him, she crept her fingers through the sand to his elbow. He felt them, seized them, grasped her hand in his, and placed an arm round her shoulders.

So they lay entwined, face to face, in their own shadow. They had no need to look at each other. They were of one mind there, in their private silence, on the little desert of sand they had occupied, where the contemplation of rock and glass grains, shell splinters, flashes of mica and quartz crystals, polished, refined, worn smooth by the winds and the nights since the dawn of time, accorded with their thoughts.

"My parents are lying like this in their coffin in Paris," he murmured. "They couldn't be separated."

"What happened?"

"They were locked together. After death all the joints . . ."

"I understand that," she said quickly; "but how?"

"They were drowned in a lake."

They bent their heads with the same movement. After a moment she whispered:

"One of them tried to save the other, is that it?"

"On the contrary."

". . ."

"He was crazed with jealousy. He dragged her down in the water."

"How do you know?"

"I was there."

"And there was nothing you could do?"

"I was eight at the time."

She hid her face in his neck and squeezed herself against him.

He pushed her away.

"It's all right, I'm not asking for pity. I've spent thirty years with that scene in the back of my mind."

She withdrew her arm.

"Sorry," she said; "that's not what I meant."

She refolded her legs under her heels and, in the shelter of her bag, lit a cigarette.

Lucas arranged himself on his back.

"Do you want one?" she asked.

He shook his head.

It was decidedly difficult to keep calm in his presence. She drew on her cigarette with trembling lips and found that it tasted of dung. Things seemed simpler, easier, for the others around them; and suddenly it was as if the sky had clouded over. Now that they had slept together, now that they'd told each other the important things, what remained but days of rain, cold mornings, restaurant dinners, silent walks in search of a cinema, endurance and improvisation? Her heart shook with a need to scream.

"You ought to put on the top of your swimsuit."

"I'll think about it."

"That style doesn't suit you."

"It's a long time since anyone has been shocked by this 'style,' as you call it, if that's what you're trying to say. Look around you; look at other people."

He straightened up, threw away her cigarette and turned her over on the sand.

"The hell with other people," he said between his teeth. "I love you. I love you so much I could die of it. And I don't want to see your breasts during the day, do you hear me? Never by daylight. You've given them to me; they're not yours. They're mine now, do you understand?"

She nodded.

He smiled, but his gaze was disturbing. His eyes in the depths of hers, he stared at her in such a profoundly disconcerting fashion that her tears shone.

"Where is it?" he asked gently. "In your bag?"

"Where's what?"

"The top of your swimsuit."

She laughed soundlessly.

"No, it's not there. You'd have to get it from the shop . . ."

"Stop laughing," he ordered; but he started laughing too. "What shop?"

"The shop where I bought the bottom half," she

said. "Just for You, in Paris. It's a simple little design they sell just as it is. Why don't you go there and give them a fright?"

They finished up laughing and rolling on the sand.

Then, the laughter tailing off, their movements growing slow and their looks heavy:

"Come on," he said; "let's go back to the hotel."

And, springing to his feet, he left her to follow him.

X V I

They lived the hours as husband and wife live years. Noon came before either had fully registered midnight. In the window frame the sailboats slowly passed on the bed's horizon; their billowing sheets extended to the white lines of foam. Mouths agape, hair awry, they slept apart despite themselves, like two people shot down and fallen any which way. Far from the parents who had brought them into the world, they used their bodies to excess. It was less than two days since they had first spoken. Closer acquaintance had told them nothing each didn't already know.

The mournful dirge of the plumbing shook the walls of the old hotel. In their absence, everything inanimate remained as if in suspension, in the order imposed by the chambermaids; air reigned supreme. Flies from the shore came and went; a shaft of swirling light glittered with dust.

People passed in the corridor. Some returned to their rooms and others left, while the slow ticking over of the two hearts under the naked skin of the bodies lying behind their partition accomplished the same ebb and flow from ventricle to ventricle. Inert, statuesque and as if disjointed, their extremities languished here and there on the sheet. Blood ran through the web of veins and ducts to the pulp of their fingers. Against the grain of the light, delicate slopes of flesh were scaled like mother-of-pearl. Thighs apart, palms open, they slowly inclined their brows. They breathed in turn as if in reply to each other; their fingers twitched.

〰〰〰

The sea was high, the beach crowded. It was that time when the situation reverses itself, the hour when no one hopes for anything more from the promise contained in the morning air; a time when one tires of the waves.

Later the grown-ups are quieter but the beach is smaller, the yellow is yellower and the blue dark-green. All along the coast the sea grows contentious; the dogs return. Then dinnertime, when the elements are relieved of the human tumult. A few solitary figures in sweaters take a last turn on the shore. They greet one another in passing and fade with the evening; and under these skies this Saturday draws to a close.

≋

They took no part in the general course of events. For hours they lay detached from the crowd, from the habits and the eternal order dictating the use of time. Since dawn, whitening fields and waking beasts and fishermen had seen them copulate, the idea of day, the idea of night, the sensations of hunger and thirst no longer ruled their lives. Sleep took them by surprise, though, and now it was two.

A solution of sand and tears congealed on their eyelids. Wrinkled by wind, they opened and closed their fists like the newly born. Life was there, apparently, with nothing but itself to bring it alive. It was there, struggling continually in a tangle of membranes, independent of love, or hope, or any other emotion. But they no more controlled their lives than frogs control the throb of their lime-green throats.

XVII

White moldings bunched up in the corners of the
ceiling . . . like meringues. Red velvet curtains
. . . the bed facing the window . . . A real room
somewhere but which . . . with François . . . that
room in Nantes . . . No, in Nantes you couldn't
hear the sea . . . Nothing moved but her still half-
seeing eyes, opening and closing peacefully in their
own silence where, little by little, as at first light in
an exotic country, she was again caught up in the
ambience of the new man she had met. Lucas!
Cabourg! The concert! All the happiness of her
present life came back to her. She turned, but the
place beside her was empty.

"Lucas . . . Lucas! . . ."

She heard herself call him in a luxurious voice

made plaintive by the expectation of seeing him run to her and cover her with kisses; but there was no reply.

"Lucas?"

She listened for a moment before getting up, then went to the bathroom and returned to stand by the bed, realizing how far she had come already from solitude. Three o'clock. The casino manager and his wife would be waiting for her in the bar. Her mother, François . . . She hadn't phoned them. To find her way back to reality wouldn't be easy, but she dived into her clothes.

In a few minutes she was running down the corridor. The elevator doors opened and suddenly, over a cardboard box of crabs, roses and ferns he was holding, they found themselves face to face.

"Where are you going?"

"I've got to meet some people," she cried, shifting from foot to foot on the landing. "I forgot all about it!"

"Who do you have to meet?" he asked, setting the box on the floor.

"I must rush. I'll tell you later," she said, disappearing into the elevator.

He blocked the doors and took her by the arm.

"Let me go, Lucas, I'm late! I'll be back shortly."

"When? . . . No!"

He pulled her out of the elevator and flung her against the wall. She hadn't gotten over her surprise when she found herself being forcibly led back down the corridor.

"Stop it! What's the matter with you?" she cried. "Stop it, you're hurting me!"

He shoved her against the door and thrust himself upon her. She felt his free hand moving between them and thought in a flash, "He's going to rape me here!" But it was only the key. They stood face to face in the bedroom, the door locked.

≋≋≋

She bunched her fist while he stood shaking. He sent the key flying across the room and slumped on the bed.

Without a word she went to pick it up, then headed for the door.

Lucas stood in her way.

"No," he said in a broken voice, "I can't agree to this."

"*I'm* the one who can't agree!"

He stuck his fists into his pockets and threw back his head.

"You don't love me," he said.

"Okay; is there anything else?"

"Why are you so disagreeable all of a sudden?"

"I have no wish to be disagreeable," she said. "On the contrary, I want us to understand each other."

"Why is your voice so harsh? I don't think you realize how hurtful your tone can be sometimes."

"It's not deliberate," she replied, containing herself. "It's the way I speak. And I repeat, I've got to meet some people."

"So what? You don't have to . . ."

"Listen," she said; "in the future, if you wish, we can decide together what appointments I should make. But this is prearranged and I have to go; now let me past."

His face was a picture of woe.

"Where's the point in this meeting now, whatever it is? Or of any other . . . I'm amazed that you're still so anxious to be there."

"And *I'm* amazed," she cried, "that you take so much upon yourself after only forty-eight hours! It concerns my work!" she added, stamping her foot. "And I . . ."

"I was going to ask you about your work, actually. Why do you want to go on with it?"

His cool assurance baffled her.

"Would you mind repeating what you just said?"

"I mean it's painful to see you involved with futile people like that. Anyone with any regard for you could only be embarrassed to see you make such a spectacle of yourself! You deserve better."

"Wait a minute, you're going too fast for me," she said, moving nearer, her eyes popping out of her head. "What do you know of such people?"

"I know them!" he yelled. "I know them inside out; I spent my childhood watching them! . . . I look at you, then I look at *them* looking at you, and it's beyond me how your mother, or even François who claims to love you . . ."

"Leave François out of this for the moment, if you don't mind."

"Okay, your mother then . . ."

"My mother too."

"I can see there's no point in talking to you."

"Oh yes there is! On the contrary! Carry on, please; it's high time we had this discussion."

He roamed about the room, making her dizzy.

"At the same time," he said, "you constantly interrupt me."

"Because you attack my very life!" she suddenly screamed, holding her head in both hands. "It's my *life*, my *life*, my *life*, my *life* . . . !"

And no doubt she would have continued to stamp the floor till she'd had a nervous breakdown, if he hadn't run and held her.

"It's my *life*," she sobbed hoarsely into his shoulder, "it's my *life* . . . Ever since I was tiny I've wanted to be a singer . . ."

He led her to the bed, sat her down, and crouched at her feet. The alarm clock showed three thirty. While she cleared her throat, sniffled, threw back her hair and hid her face from him, he waited, kneading her hand until she relented.

"The trouble is I've stuck you on a pedestal," he murmured. "I've idealized you, placed you higher than . . ."

A last sigh escaped her, then all signs of it disappeared. Raising her eyes, she found Lucas smiling mournfully at her.

"Do you want to phone?"

"Yes."

"Is it important? Who is it?"

"The manager of the casino."

"Where were you to meet him?"

"In the bar downstairs."

"I suppose it would be polite to let him know . . . You're in no state now to . . ."

"No, I'm in no state."

He lifted the phone and placed it on her knee. She picked up the receiver.

"Do you know what you're going to say?"

"No, not exactly," she mumbled, hanging up again.

"I'll do it for you if you like . . ."

"No . . . No, I'd better do it."

"Perhaps you're right . . . Well then, you've only to say: 'Monsieur, I'm terribly sorry to have kept you waiting. Something came up at the last minute. I hope you won't hold it against me. I'll be in touch again as soon as possible . . .' That should do; can you remember it? Do you want me to write it down?"

"No, it's okay," she said. "But . . ."

"But what? . . . Tell me."

"Would you mind waiting in the bathroom? I can't do it with you listening."

"Of course," he said, getting to his feet. "Take your time."

≋≋≋

After a moment he reappeared at the open bathroom door.

"All clear?"

She was stretched out on the bed, staring at the ceiling. He came over, removed the phone, and slid down beside her.

"Perhaps you should ring François too?"

"I did."

"Good; and what did he say?"

"Nothing."

XVIII

Her body rose and leaned over Lucas; her voice said, I have to go now, I'll probably see you again this evening. No, really, it's true, she said, I'm singing again tonight at nine, I'd love you to be there . . . Her body withdrew, crossed the room, passed through the door, went off down the corridor and ran and ran up the road and her hand grasped the doorknob and her heart leapt to hear Bear barking and her legs took the stairs four at a time and her voice cried Mummy, François, are you there? And she heard her beloved mother's voice answering Ah, here's Blanche. Blanche, have you had lunch? We're in the back drawing room. People have been phoning for you. Would you like some tea, something to eat, yes, an omelette and a bath and clean clothes and a bit of news and gossip and laughter and I've taken in a stitch in your bodice, dear, and oh Mummy I love him! I love him! We spent the night together, Mummy! You are my mother, hug me tight, I haven't washed, I haven't eaten, I haven't slept, I vomited, I cried the whole morning, I can't think straight anymore, I don't know what to do, the concert starts in five hours' time, I haven't seen the manager, I've failed myself, I've failed François who was so happy to put us up, I promised to help him pick cherries this morning, I promised to go with him to see Madame Berreby and how is her son who was so sick and how are the dahlias I planted at Easter, did Brice and Maryvonne sleep okay in the downstairs bedroom, how have you all been since I left you in the dark so long ago? I was young and foolish, I wanted to sing, I wanted to please and surprise you! I was still attached to my "secret self." My one source of strength returns, I remember the magic of your words as you sat on the edge of my bed one evening: "You are born with her; she lives in the depths of you. She's the one who will make you suffer, make you dream and make you sing. Take care of her; protect her; she is fragile, easy to kill. They'll try to take her from you, but you mustn't give her away. You can give your time, your body, your love; but you must never give away your secret self." . . . Mummy, he's touched my secret self! I can't hear her now, I can't feel her, and my rage has died with her little voice . . . He scorned you, he scorned me, I couldn't answer him, I'm weak with euphoria. All I want now is him, him, it's the same pleasant fatigue, the same fulfillment, it may not make me famous but it's better than singing! He's right . . . Why get up when we'll be lying down again in a few hours? Why all this dressing up and running around? Why wander from town to town and weep into an old pillow at night? Why seek out auditions and humiliations, why spend my nights and my Sundays transcribing the score of a happiness I am obliged to invent while others live it, why are sky, seasons, stars, men, rivers and birds only there for me as material for my crappy songs that don't know how to make that happiness work, why must my least emotions be public property, why sacrifice my life to people I don't even know, why, oh why can I not belong to *me*? It's all because of my "secret self"! She's the one who prevents me being a normal woman, she's the one who made me leave François, she's the one who makes me leave everyone, except you and my solitude, she's the one who stands between Lucas and me, who provoked our first row, she's the one who appears as soon as I fall in love, I shit on my "secret self," she won't make me leave *this* man. It's summer! The hell with fame! The hell with casino managers! I want to be his wife! I have only sung until now in order to meet him! I've only gone through what I've gone through in order, one day, to be loved as he loves me! He is splendid and fierce, he understands me beyond the need for words, like us he loves what is beautiful and pure; he is perfect, he . . .

"There's something bothering you," he said. "I can feel it."

"Not at all, I'm fine, but . . . Didn't I see you just now with a great big crab?"

"Two crabs, you mean. Yes; but where are they? I think they hid in the corridor. Wait till I get my hands on them!"

She burst out laughing as he leapt from the bed.

"Nobody leaves you like that, eh, not even a crab?" she called, watching him dash to the door.

"Ah no; no one has ever left me like that, the little buggers!"

He fought with the locked door in his haste to get out.

"Ah, ah!"

He turned round.

She waved the key with two fingers.

"Ah, ah, ah!"

Head down, he returned frowning to the bed.

"Who are these crabs exactly?" she asked. "What time were you supposed to meet them? I'm amazed, after what has happened between us . . ."

He pounced on her.

"No, no!"

While she laughed and struggled, he worked his fingers one by one toward the key. She rolled on her side.

"What do you say? What do you say first?" she demanded, on the brink of defeat.

"Please . . . my love . . . my kingdom for a . . ."

"Take it."

Out in the corridor, he heard her chortling with pleasure.

X I X

She was tidying up the bed when he came back with the cardboard box. They ordered a white wine, salad, toast and strawberries. While Blanche placed the roses in a vase, Lucas produced newspapers, chocolate, then a little dress of silk crêpe you could hold in one hand. He let it glide over the back of an armchair.

"There you are," said he without ceremony.

"Where did you get that? What is it?"

"It's so you can change if you want to."

"It's lovely! . . . But you shouldn't have, Lucas," she said in a reproachful tone, holding it up to the light. "I've got all I need at home!"

She heard him go to the bathroom; then the buzz of an electric razor. There was a knock at the door.

She hid the crabs and opened it to admit an expressionless young man whom she led to the coffee table.

"You work in the bar?" she whispered. "Do you know Pierrot Colin, the lighting man in the casino?"

"Yes, he's downstairs; I've just been talking to him."

She motioned him to speak quietly.

"Listen, I was supposed to meet him at four and I couldn't make it . . . Would you mind very much telling him Blanche says she'll wait for him this evening at six in the hall of the casino itself? Blanche, six o'clock: okay?"

"Of course, I'll tell him," he murmured.

She thanked him with her eyes, signed the bill he handed her, and the young man withdrew.

"Aren't you finished yet?" she called.

She laid the table, set out the crabs on plates and put the tray aside. Perching for a moment on an armchair, it occurred to her to snap the head off a rose, which she placed between the claws of Lucas's crab; then she sat back on a cushion.

It was nearly five. A golden glow lit up the red crab shells and the crystals around the rim of the ice-bucket. Seagulls hurtled past the window; then Lucas, looking grim, returned from the bathroom.

"What's the matter?" she exclaimed.

He sat down without a word and started pouring

the wine. But his eyes, like those of a detective, made a furtive inspection of everything in the vicinity, coming to rest on the proffered rose.

"Why did you interfere with my flowers?"

She was speechless.

"I asked you a question. Didn't you hear me?"

"It's something else, Lucas; you can't . . . You can't really be making a scene about the rose."

"I can't imagine why people damage flowers."

"Since the flowers were from you, I supposed they were for *me*—stupidly, I admit," she said, sitting up; "and I apologize . . . But for you to spoil this excellent meal for me on such a trivial pretext, that I will not tolerate."

And, picking up the rose, she tossed it out the window.

"There now, eat up!" she added drily, taking up her fork.

≋≋≋≋

Silence fell between them. They paid no further attention to anything but the cracking of crab-shells and the sucking of claws. Lucas refilled their glasses regularly. Their strength returned, and with it renewed confidence. Face to face, each thought of the other and their annoyance abated. They knew themselves in accord. On that basis, they came to reflect on what it would be like to break up, though not alarming themselves with the thought that it would be the one necessary condition for rediscovering the peace they had known before they knew each other . . . When they had finished eating Lucas rose and fetched his tobacco. He handed Blanche a damp cloth for her fingers, and lit her cigarette with her gold lighter as if thoroughly content.

"Now tell me," said she morosely, "what was the moody look about?"

He came and sat at the foot of her chair, and she placed a hand on his head while he filled his pipe.

"Nothing at all," he said. "Don't give it another thought."

"Come on, you can tell me now."

"It's not important, I tell you."

"But I need to *know*."

"It's nothing really; just something you let slip."

"When?"

"A while back."

". . . when I said, 'Nobody leaves you like that'?"

"No, later; when I gave you the dress."

She puffed at her cigarette and tried to remember.

"I didn't thank you properly?"

"No, it's not that."

"Tell me, Lucas; it will be so much easier. Honestly, I can't remember . . . What did I say?"

"You said, 'at home.' "

X X

Far off at the end of her arm, her hand felt the roundness of Lucas's skull, the obstetrical bumps, the boiling tumult of the brain beneath, and combed his hair with languorous fingers. The fact of her hand on his head was sufficient testimony to her present feelings. At the same time, it pleased her to consider him from above. Index and ring fingers a little raised, the other fingers hanging loose, it was the hand not of a pianist at a ghostly keyboard but of a woman in love. But, seeing it white among the black hair, she found something deathly about it and drew it away.

"You see?" he said. "I knew you would turn against me."

"Oh Lucas . . . ! Surely I can be free in my movements . . . ?"

He rose and strode around the room in silence.

"What is it *this* time? What have I said now?"

"Nothing; you just keep doing the same things," he said in a dull voice. "It's probably not your fault. Obviously you've never been in love."

"What gives you the right to say that? . . ."

"All these phrases that spring to your lips: 'at home,' 'be free' . . . And in five minutes you'll be telling me, 'I have to phone' or 'I've got to meet some people' . . ."

"Precisely," she said.

"What?"

"Yes, Lucas, I *do* have to meet some people. What can I do about it? I'm here to work, you seem to have deliberately forgotten that . . ."

"But do *I* work?" he yelled. "Do *I* insult *you* in this way? . . . *I* could work if I wanted to! I've got work too, you know!"

He leapt at his files.

"Look, look at that!"

He threw sheaves of paper, which fell around her like rain.

". . . 'Language as a Disease' . . . 'The Cry for Help' . . . 'Draft Outline for a New Translation of Original Sound' . . . There you are, see? Plenty of work! . . . 'Last Memories of the Water' . . . 'Toward a Second Explanation of the Silence of God'

. . . There you are, look at that! Chapter eight! . . . 'Retention and Survival of Swear Words' . . . Do you think that isn't work?"

"Stop it, Lucas! Stop it, stop it!"

She ran everywhere, gathering up the pages, and took him by the arm; but he went on gesticulating with the other.

". . . What about this? '*Mama*, the First and Last Intelligible Word' . . . See? . . . 'Study of an Adult Regression to Stammering' . . . 'Words, the Open Wounds of Silence' . . . See? It's not difficult! . . . 'On the Optimism of Leibnitz' . . . Well, is it work or not? And do *I* bore *you* to death with all that?"

He swept the rest aside with the back of his hand and collapsed in an armchair. She threw herself against him.

"But I'm *interested* in your work," she murmured; "*very* interested . . . We've had so little time! Until now I haven't dared ask you about it, I was waiting for you to talk about it yourself, for it to happen of its own accord. I realize I was wrong . . ."

"Go on; go and see whoever you have to see."

He hid his face behind his arms, as he had when she surprised him in his mad fit at two o'clock that morning.

She kissed his cheek.

"I won't be long," she whispered and, falling quite naturally into the controlled breathing she used against stage fright, added in a firm voice:

"I've got to see the lighting man from the casino about this evening's concert; but I'll be back by seven. I'd like you to see me perform. I'd sing better than last night if I knew you were in the hall. I'd sing for *you* . . . We'll go together and come back here together, okay? And then we can talk; we can take our time and get to know each other . . ."

He said nothing.

She planted a last kiss on his cheek, got slowly to her feet, stepped back, grabbed her bag, and fled.

≈≈≈≈

There you are—shit!—every last one of them does that with doors . . . take it easy . . . Always slamming, always turning handles, always disappearing with a frown and a busy air, whether to go out, to wash, to cook, pretending there's smoke, pretending there's steam, always everywhere their hands fluttering around doors to open them, to close them, women one behind the other to infinity, doors banging all day long and when the doors are open they want them closed, but when they're closed, ah, when they're closed, then they want them open! And later, when the doors complain, they shout that that door's dragging again, René, for heaven's sake do something about it, it's driving me crazy! . . . That door keeps creaking, Lucas, I've asked you a hundred times . . . I can hear it shaking at night at the end of the garden! But when the doors are silent, just hear them remark in a desolate voice, I didn't hear you come in this evening . . . the hell with it . . . *Their* doors would be planed, oiled and rehung, draughts excluded by means of cloth flaps, the kitchen aired and modernized, Antoine and Son will attend to the veranda, windows will be opened, eiderdowns shaken out in the sun, once the grass is cut, the nettles cleared and the currant bushes tidied up, in no time at all the roses, wisteria and snapdragons will revive . . . As for the wood, you'd better see Puicesseau about that, his phone number should still be on the list behind the kitchen door, she would lose no time discovering who was who, crossing off those who had died, getting new help from the creamery office, distinguishing rain water from spring water, setting mousetraps, checking the weathervane if clouds appeared in the mountains, women know things like that instinctively when they move into a new house . . . She would have her own bathroom, and a bedroom to herself, so she would feel "free" to write her letters and do her nails, perhaps the corner bedroom with the best bed though sometimes the wind carries the honking of Madame Vivien's geese to that side of the house, if she still has geese . . . She can have her mother to stay, even François if she wishes, dust off the checkerboard and the backgammon table, bring up the vintage wines from the cellar, take out the dresses and shoes she likes from the wardrobes, with things back to normal the sewing basket smelling of sweets, the table mats, the silver service, the walking sticks and sun hats in the porch and all the forgotten treasures will reappear. We'll get the Buick out of the garage, go find Emily in her village if she hasn't married or even if she has, drive them back to the house, she and Emily will take to each other at once, Emily seeing herself as she was when she was a girl going into service, she'll show her where the sheets are kept, in which room coffee is served, tell her what days the co-op and the fishmonger call, explain that cider and champagne are delivered directly to the kitchen, that the deliveryman gets a drink when he's carried in the crates, but doesn't sit down. Emily will take up her ironing again when the alarm clock rings in the kitchen, and no sooner will the first child be on its feet than she'll make it a dish of pears and rice though without repeating "Come out from under my legs" . . . They might give a reception for those who had taken the trouble to follow the hearse as far as the highway. The old people who walked their bicycles by the handlebars up the forest slope in the evening heat amid the odor of wood smoke would no longer be of this world, but to amuse her there will be Madame Chambellan's children with whom it would be easy to renew acquaintance since they had always taken care to send him cards announcing their weddings and the births that resulted from them . . . No doubt the little Martineaus will still be there, and they can show her their butterfly collection . . . And if she misses her singing, it will be easy to go to La Bourboule or to Mont-Doré, to drive her to one or another of those resorts, there was no lack of casinos, and the managers, out of respect for the family and all the money the Boyenvals had thrown away at their tables, will be honored to have her perform some Saturday evening or whenever she pleases . . .

He rose, paced about the room, paused at the window, and left it again reluctantly. Were it not for the consciousness of his own presence which accompanied every movement, reminding him that he was alone, nothing would have bothered him. She had said she would be back, but he remembered nothing of what exactly she was doing or of what she had said they would do together this evening. He was content simply to wait for her a little longer; she would tell him again when she returned . . . He started putting his things in order, then rang reception to ask if they wouldn't mind making up his bill. It was a fine evening for a drive; they would be in Auvergne before midnight. He took his shaving kit and, still scratching the corners of his memory for who it was she had to see and why, he went into the bathroom.

He remembered then what she had said; but it was nearly an hour before he was struck by the full force of her extraordinary announcement.

X X I

~~~~~~~~~~~~~

There was green, pink, ultramarine and dark gray, a golden glory lancing the cotton-wool clouds; in the cumulus a baroque complexity beyond comprehension where cupids might be released in the heavens this evening, as in the convent gardens at Corpus Christi. What with all this unfolding of colors and shapes, it was in fact a sky to make one think of becoming a nun . . . She ran, head thrown back, laughing at nothing in particular, at peace with her mother, with François, with herself; with a toothbrush and a T-shirt for the night in her bag, she ran on winged feet. It was nearly seven.

Driven by an excess of vitality that puffed out her chest, she breasted the stream of men and women returning to their homes, everything catching her eye simultaneously: the gleam of a bicycle, the fatigue of a face, a stick of barley sugar in the dust, the fall of a child, the aerobatics of swifts in a panic of midges. She shared all these worlds in a flash, moved almost to tears by the innocence of her fellow creatures carefully carrying their personal belongings, leading exhausted children home to bed while she ran toward her destiny . . . Any more of this and she wouldn't have time to tell him all she had seen in the streets this evening, all that was taking place on earth so that the world might be beautiful and sing its blessed vicissitudes, as she would presently do, in public and before the man she loved.

≈≈≈≈≈

Drunk with fresh air, light and excited anticipation, she ran up the steps of the Grand Hotel, reached the fourth floor, and walked calmly down the corridor to room 420.

As in a strange dream, the key was in the door; but behind it was only darkness.

A hot, stifling silence engulfed her as she stepped into the room. Doors and windows were closed, blinds lowered, curtains drawn. Still half-blinded by the sunset, she groped her way forward. Tables and chairs were obliterated by a feverish wriggling of yellow insects before her wide-open eyes. A strong animal smell rose from the bed. An indeterminate presence other than her own dominated the atmosphere and made the place immense. She murmured:

"Are you asleep?"

And stood waiting.

Gradually, on the whiteness of a pillow, a dark shock of hair materialized.

"Lucas? . . . Here I am."

The covers moved, the sheets rose and subsided; two eyes shone in the darkness.

"What's wrong?" she whispered.

She drew nearer and sat on the edge of the bed.

"Lucas, answer me, I hardly know you like this . . . You frighten me . . . Are you sick?"

"Yes . . . No . . . ," he said in a scarcely audible voice. "I don't know what's the matter with me."

"But what do you feel? Are you in pain?"

He emitted a long sigh which she didn't dare interrupt.

"I hear noises . . . ," he said.

"What noises?"

"I don't know . . . Like running water . . ."

"I can't hear anything," she said; "but I can look in the bathroom if you like. Maybe you left a tap running . . ."

She stood up.

"I've already looked, several times . . . It's not that."

She sat down again.

"Can't you speak normally?" she asked.

"I'm trying . . . I can't make myself . . ."

She drew back the sheet and saw that he was fully dressed. He covered himself up again immediately.

"You know, it's still lovely outside."

"What time . . . ?"

"After seven. Half past, even, I should think . . . Shall I put on the light? I want to look at the clock."

"No . . . No, I'm cold . . . I'm cold . . . Get into bed with me."

She let her hand fall.

"One thing's clear," she said sadly; "you won't be coming with me to the show tonight."

"Come here," he shivered. "I have to get warm first."

"Yes, and I've got to get undressed, get dressed again, redo my hair . . . No, Lucas, I haven't time! . . . I came here to fetch you; I thought you'd be ready! It's not very considerate of you . . . I go on stage in an hour! It's hard enough to concentrate . . ."

"I'm cold, I tell you . . . Come here . . ."

And she heard a sound like a mouse crying.

"Oh, Lucas darling, are you crying?"

She fell on top of him, real tears wetting her cheeks.

"Why are you crying? There really *is* something wrong, isn't there? What is it? What's happened to my love?"

"Just for a minute, then I'll come with you; that's all I ask."

"Okay; but promise . . . Close your eyes, I'm going to turn on the lamp for a minute. There. It's twenty to eight. Promise me that in twenty minutes we'll both be up."

"Yes," he said.

She took off her dress, laid it flat on the carpet, and got into bed.

≋≋≋

They didn't move; they didn't speak; they couldn't see each other; they hardly breathed. Their arms and legs retained their first position; their muscles remained taut in the anxiety of the moment. They held each other tight, each waiting to see what the other would do.

It was Lucas's room, Lucas's bed, his arms, his smell and his skin; she recognized it, she had talked to him about it and he had replied. It was Lucas and yet it wasn't him.

"Why are you acting so strangely?" he asked.

"I'm not acting—"

"Well, why don't you hold me tight?"

"I'm holding you as tight as I can . . . there, see?"

"But you're remote; you're not really with me."

"I'm here beside you," she whispered. "You're imagining things. Close your eyes and stop tormenting us."

He obeyed.

But a moment later he said in a dull voice:

"If I asked you to hold me, there, in your hands, would you do it?"

"Oh Lucas," she cried, sitting up, "this is impossible! What's the matter with you?"

"Answer me . . . I need to know . . . Would you do it?"

"No, I wouldn't! Certainly not; you know perfectly well. And if there's any more of this I'm getting up right away."

He freed a hand, then a leg, before she realized what he was up to. He stretched out on top of her and moved up and down with determined movements.

"Lucas!"

He shut her mouth with his, tore off her panties, and thrust himself inside her.

Releasing her lips, he heard only a bubbling of saliva. Releasing her legs and arms, he felt them close around him once again. The loins he had forced compelled him with an even greater force. Rage, a mute rage full of grace, had taken hold of his victim. He hadn't enough surface to his body now to cover this pale, moving spider which grew, which spread around him in the darkness, swung him between its limbs, mingled him with its softness, extorting from him his innermost reserves . . . Already half-paralyzed, he no longer knew which way to turn to please her. She clung to his hair, hoisted him by the armpits, set him back on her stomach, vanished into a pillow and reappeared in a fury; then everything stopped, and as she rocked him he heard, as if from a distance, her irresponsible laugh.

He remained suspended, inert and vigilant; and she too lay still.

"That was great," he said softly; "that was great . . . Just the thing before you sing."

"I haven't finished!" she flashed angrily.

"No . . . hey, you mustn't!" he protested. "No . . . please, there isn't time . . ."

But already she'd taken hold of him again, sobbing the hell with it, fuck them all, the hell with it! . . .

XXII

Around the gardens in front of the Grand Hotel, cars cruised in search of parking space. Doors slammed. Talking among themselves, women in long dresses stood waiting in the breeze. Daylight lingered in the green of the lawns; the salt evening air lay thickly on silk scarves and windowpanes. High heels and patent leather clattered across the expanse of tarmac. Men in black and white, keys jingling, collected their wives' shawls. Respectable, fragrant, full-length against the sky, confident figures appeared on all sides. Bronzed, relaxed faces mimed silent greetings, recognizing one another at à distance . . . All over town waiters were summoned, desserts ordered, cigars lit, bills added up, arrangements made for supper at midnight, and everyone made their way to the casino.

≈≈≈≈

Some distance above it, in a stifling bedroom, the singer who was supposed to open the concert slept in the arms of a man with his trousers around his knees. Outside, posters bearing her name, black on yellow, stirred in the night wind. Her name was taken up and whispered from person to person, it was theirs in exchange for a ticket which gave them also the right to a seat and a drink. The hall began to fill up. Breathing in unison, the two slumbering heads communed together. His nose in her hair, his mouth open, the sea whispered in the shells of his ears. Nothing and nobody could harm them.

A breeze touched his shoulder and he woke.

"Blanche!"

He switched on the lamp, rolled out of bed, shook her, and ran to open the blind.

"Blanche! Get up!"

He brought her a glass of water, placed her dress on the bed, got out her hairbrush, surrounded her with everything he could think of, and leaned against her.

"Don't . . . move," she breathed.

"Yes, move, and fast; you have to sing! . . ."

Her eyes were enormous. Slowly they opened on another world, which seized her own and wouldn't let it be.

"Oh my God, what can I do to help?" pleaded Lucas. "Do you have cleansing cream in your bag?"

He emptied the makeup box, found cotton wool and a tube of something he squeezed into the hollow of his hand. White stuff squirted out; he spread it on her face, as he had seen girls do, and rubbed it off with the cotton wool.

"The blue . . . bottle . . ."

He started again with the blue bottle, stuffed several squares of chocolate into her mouth, washed it down with whiskey, slid one arm under her neck and the other under her thighs, and set her on her feet.

"Right, can you manage?"

While he was getting her dress, she swayed crookedly toward the bathroom.

"Where are you going?" he cried, grabbing her.

She looked at him imploringly.

"To wash?"

"No, no, you haven't time! Quick, lift your arms!"

While she buttoned her dress from top to bottom, he tore at her hair with the brush. Her shoes waited, pointing in the direction she would take; leaning on Lucas, all she had to do was insert her feet. He snapped two fasteners shut and pushed her into the corridor.

"Go on!" he cried, throwing into her bag anything feminine he found lying on the bed. "Ring for the elevator!"

He reached the stairhead before her.

"It's going to be all right," he said, more anxious than she, as they went down in the elevator. "You're beautiful, exciting, you radiate sexuality, you're visibly happy," he went on without pausing for breath . . . "That's important, you know, it's something an audience feels . . . The people right at the back, you're going to wow them, right? And I'll be there to hear you, my eyes won't leave you for a second, okay?"

The doors opened. He took her hand and they dived across the hall. At the mouth of the corridor, the little troop led by her mother and François, on their way to the reception desk in search of a certain Lucas, recoiled in surprise . . . People opened doors for them, crowded into corners for them, flattened themselves against walls to let them pass. Look, it's Blanche! She's late! This way, this way! Gisèle! Help her get dressed, Gisèle! A girl took Blanche's things from him and Blanche let go his hand. François and her mother took over; two, three, five people jostled him, and then he was alone in front of a locked door.

≋≋≋

He went and mingled with the late arrivals crowding around the entrance of the concert hall, where he presented his ticket. A thick-looking bouncer type blocked his way.

"Sorry, m'sieur; can't let you in like that."

"But I've a ticket: here. What more do you want?"

"A tie . . . A jacket at least, if you have one."

Lucas clenched his fists but contained himself.

"I'm a friend of the artist; it was I who brought her here. To tell you the truth, I haven't had time to change . . ."

"It's the rule," said the bouncer, his fat, stupid eyes turning away.

Between missing Blanche's entrance and not getting in at all, the decision was a simple one. As fast as his legs could carry him, he retraced his steps to room 420, grabbed a jacket, and presently stood once more at the door of the hall. The lights were on already, an impatient clapping had broken out here and there.

"Do you have the time?" he gasped, sweating, to the bouncer.

"Do you have a ticket?"

He emptied his pockets, smacked his clothes all over: no, he had no ticket.

"Hang on, here it is," said the bouncer mildly, in the best of humor. "It's nine fifteen. What with you not having a tie, I'd rather you went in when the lights is down. But it's an improvement; in you go."

"You, however, are beyond improvement," said Lucas and, content with having put the man in his place, he took refuge among the tables.

It would have been fun to insult a few more people, but no one took any notice of him. There was nothing to do but wait, his hands between his knees. To have been master of events only a short time before, to have held the fate of the concert in his hands, to have been an intimate of the artist, a relation even, and to have finished up so soon among these parasites, left in his heart the bitter residue of unrecognized initiative. When two perfectly pleasant people asked him if he would mind moving his chair slightly, he refused. The whole evening, from the very existence of the show to the chaos which must be reigning in the wings, was entirely his own creation. It was thanks to him that the two morons who had asked him to move his chair would have the privilege of seeing his wife appear, if they'd only sit down and shut up.

XXIII

Even had she produced no sound, Blanche with her demeanor, her violin, the line of her dress trembling like a leaf in the wind, Blanche silent, one leg at an angle in that unique way she had, would already have been a considerable performance in herself. Had she doubted it for an instant, he could have reassured her on that score without hesitation . . . And he longed to say to her, "A few notes from your mouth and I am transported to a lost winter palace in the East, flying to the stars with a raging whore; for this is great art, you manipulate your audience exactly as you please . . ." Brimming with love and admiration, he was the first to leave when the applause began . . . So that she might excuse him, in the presence of her mother and François, for the anxiety his negligence had caused them, he would order champagne; then, once she had lost no time getting ready, he would drive her to dinner in the Auge country . . . But, opening the door which led backstage, he heard shouting and crying.

It had to do with some lighting effect that hadn't gone off as intended, a cramp and a silly posture, a vibrato that stuck in the throat, a mechanical delivery, two songs omitted altogether, a sequence without rhyme or reason, stage effects sketchily executed, various inadequacies. What about the tremolo in the first piece they had rehearsed so carefully? It had sounded like something in an amateur talent contest: no life, no art, no warmth, no feeling, no vitality, nothing! At this point in a career, it was important never to underestimate an audience . . . You want to be a singer? Oh yes, *ma non troppo!* Well, if it means acting like that, very well, but it would have been better to give up before making a travesty of yourself!

Taking stock of the situation, he hid in an alcove. Blanche had a downright, heartfelt way of crying which no attempt at consolation could alleviate. Her mother should know that, being responsible for it. Two men's voices murmured in the background; the dressing room emitted a strong light. How many were there, exactly, in that little room? He began to doubt if his opinion, as a member of the audience, would really be welcome; on the other hand, his position as lover and protector required that he should not leave her in the hands of her tormentors. But, thinking of her, of himself, and of the future, he decided that discretion was the better part of valor, and went to wait for her at the exit.

It was a veritable committee which appeared, half an hour later, at the top of the lighted steps. Down below, alone in the dark, he could see through the glass doors without being seen. Blanche, framed by her bodyguards, came down the steps toward him, wearing the dress he had put on with his own hands, her eyes lowered, not looking for him. An unknown man held her by the elbow; François carried the violin. Her mother, out in front, tried to disguise her distress. All were silent and grave.

Arms dangling, Lucas emerged from the shadows. François saw him first and whispered something to Blanche, but she didn't look up. François increased the pace, her mother took her by the other elbow and drew her aside, and like five oxen yoked together the whole bunch swerved away and vanished into the night.

"Blanche!" cried Lucas.

He ran after them, stopped, shouted:

"Blanche, I want to talk to you!"

The group continued to move away; but a figure detached itself and François approached. He came as close as civilization permits; he had the same clear gaze as his wife.

"I've been asked to tell you," he said politely, "that Blanche doesn't wish to speak to you. She needs to rest. Please leave her alone."

And off he went again.

≋≋≋≋

My name is Lucas Boyenval. My name is Lucas Boyenval. My name is Lucas Boyenval. You know only my first name and my body. One day of talk, one day of love, and you send word that you're tired. I know how strong you are. I know how passionate you can be. It's not true, it wasn't your idea. I don't understand, but never mind.

My name is Lucas Boyenval. I was alive long before you. I have been waiting for you. You have had the vulgarity to marry. You have made a mockery of love. Now you make a mockery of friendship with your shrimp of a husband. I wasn't brought up like that, but never mind.

My name is Lucas Boyenval. For thirty years now I've been looking for you. I chose you. I expect you're afraid, you enlist your mother, your husband, conventional morality and all that shit in order to evade me. But they won't suffice.

My name is Lucas Boyenval. With me, no singing. No working. No cooking. No talking. No phoning your mother. No people to meet. No need for self-expression, self-realization, self-fulfillment.

With me you don't relax, you don't wash, you don't get out of bed, you keep silent and breathe.

My name is Lucas Boyenval. Girls think I'm mad. They've got nothing but broad daylight between their legs, they pour scent all over themselves and that's supposed to turn you on; but *you* smell of sweat and new-mown hay, you've got a bird in your throat and your throat in your cunt. I like that.

My name is Lucas Boyenval. I'm not a sociable man. I have no family and no need of friends. I find happiness difficult. I haven't cried for thirty years. Tonight you made me cry. I'll change, just for you.

My name is Lucas Boyenval. I recognize you, you are my wife. I offer you pleasure, I offer you life, to take you further.

My name is Lucas Boyenval. I am two men. It's the other one who loves you.

My name is Lucas Boyenval.

I expect you to be there, to *stay* there, I expect you to bear my child. I expect to see you white-haired and still a woman. I am already older than my father.

My name is Lucas Boyenval.

Lucas Boyenval, born of a promiscuous mother, can no longer wait.

Lucas Boyenval, born of mortal parents, will not be abandoned a second time.

Lucas Boyenval, son of a murderer, has not yet given up.

153 ≈≈≈≈

But Lucas Boyenval is kind.

He understands that his wife needs rest. That's all right; he'll have some supper, then go to bed. He won't sleep, though, he won't cry, and presently she'll be back.

XXIV

The crater, the eyes . . . Tonight, amazingly, the moon re-created *gratis*, for him alone, the stage face of Blanche. It was a sign. Upright and unafraid, he felt authoritative once more. This same moon had bathed, with its green light, shepherds and flocks in the days of Jesus Christ; it kept vigil on the lake in the forest where it had watched the last convulsions of his parents; it was the same moon, a little bashed in, which had seen them separated this evening. She would be able to see it too, despite the flight of chubby angels from the west that clung to the halo, wherever and with whomever she was hiding. It was as nearly full as made no difference: women like that, lacking confidence, sometimes carried one shoulder higher than the other . . . But he recognized her. She was the same midsummer moon, harlotry in one eye and all innocence in the other, now game for anything, now quite impassive like Emily in her silent moods, like the grocery woman who gave short change, like Anne-Clarisse who would hide behind a smile . . . It won't happen a second time. If Blanche didn't open the door in the morning, an hour from now, this very minute, he would throw himself from the window.

A draft touched his shoulder and raised the hem of the curtains. The sea crashed furiously twice on the shore and was silent. The faint squeak of a floorboard told him she was there. He listened to her intermittent breathing.

"I've come to tell you . . . ," she began.

"I know; close the door."

Blanche did so and remained on the threshold. While he still had his back turned she studied him rapidly, memorizing his long white-trousered legs in the dim light, the irregular creases, the bulge of his thighs, the bulge of a hand in his pocket, and the terrible shining contours of his bare chest in the moonlight, where every tendon, every muscle, gleamed and quivered with vigilance.

"I've come back to tell you above all not to—"

"Don't worry; I love you."

"Let me speak, Lucas; it's hard enough as it is. I haven't the strength—"

"I'm asking you no questions."

"No, but I'm asking you to listen to *me* for a minute. I can't and won't leave you without—"

"Who's telling you to leave me? François?"

"No, not François, and besides that's not the point. I simply want to explain why I—"

"I find your husband quite likable, only the cut of his clothes is a little pretentious. It's not usual among traveling salesmen."

She stood nonplussed.

"François is anything but pretentious," she said.

"I'm not talking about him; I'm talking about his clothes."

"I think you're really talking to prevent *me* from talking. I'm exhausted, I'm going home to bed. I'll leave a letter for you at the desk tomorrow."

"I, I, I . . . ," he called after her. "There really is no limit to your egotism."

"You'll have my explanation tomorrow. Good night, Lucas."

"Tomorrow I won't be here," he said, turning slowly in her direction.

She was taken aback, but recovered quickly.

"What time are you leaving?"

"Right away."

Blanche kept silence, and Lucas let it last. He didn't move. Her face was hidden by her hair. She wasn't carrying her bag, only a bunch of keys, as if she had just slipped out to buy a loaf of bread. Her arms were white in the shadows.

"You're wearing the dress I gave you," he said softly.

"Yes . . ."

He moved carefully toward the chest of drawers.

"You left your cigarettes here. I put them aside for you."

He handed them to her.

"Why don't you take one and sit down for a bit? I've got a few minutes to spare."

Blanche let go the doorknob. She no longer knew how to cross this room. Constrained more than invited, she placed one foot in front of the other until she reached the first armchair, while he looked for glasses and something to drink.

Her chair faced the window. He slid into the other. A little round table stood between them. Moonlight glanced from her knees and collarbone. Only the occasional glow of her cigarette gave a touch of warmth to this feminine set piece.

"Who writes the words of your songs?"

"My mother wrote one; the rest are my own."

"The ones I heard," he began, "struck me as quite remarkable. I found myself wondering how you could know so much . . . You're an unusual combination of paganism and . . ."

"Please," she murmured. "I'm delighted you like my songs; but we haven't much time, and I'd like to talk to you . . ."

"Don't be so mean-spirited!" he shouted with sudden rage. "Never mind the time! We'll take as much time as we need."

More gently he added:

"Haven't we always?"

"Yes, but it's already very late and time to say good-bye," she replied. "So please, let's get it over with. I didn't want you to have a bad night because of me, and I wanted to tell you—"

"You can tell me on the way!" he said, getting up nervously. "You're quite right, there's no point in waiting another night. Here, put on this sweater, it'll be cold; we'll go right now."

He himself slipped one arm into a sleeve of his linen jacket and, the other hanging down his back, went around the room, his wallet in his hand, making incoherent gestures and remarks.

Blanche rose and flung the sweater aside.

"Keep your sweater!" she cried.

"You're making a mistake," he said without turning round. "It's cold at night on a motorbike, and we've got mountains to cross . . . Where did I put my handkerchief? You must have put it away, try to remember . . . Never mind, we won't find it, there are drawers full of them down there . . ."

"What do you mean, 'down there'?" she yelled.

"I have a big house in the country, lovely and dark; didn't I tell you? It's warm in the winter and cool in the summer . . . Often I think: that house is alive, it creaks, it calls and I'm not there . . . Just wait till you see it . . ."

And retracing his steps at random he bumped into Blanche, who was trying to slip out unobserved.

"What are you doing?"

He switched on the ceiling light, dazzling her.

"I'm just going outside," she said, backing away. "Didn't you say we were leaving?"

She saw his upper lip trembling. Pupils enlarged, forehead glistening with a fine sweat, he advanced upon her until she stumbled against a radiator.

"That's not true, you're not just going outside. You're lying to me now. You're not just going outside, I haven't said to yet, you're leaving without me! Why are you lying, since when have you lied to me?"

"Since when have women been detained by force?" she cried, panic-stricken. "You can't do what you're doing! You don't really believe I'm going to follow you just like that, wherever you're going? I don't even know you! We spend a night in bed together; so what? What are you anyway, a café pickup, not even a friend, are you sick or something . . . ?"

She made resolutely for the door; but her hair was seized and so fiercely pulled that her mouth opened in pain and she raised a hand. With a crunch of bone the back of her head came down between her shoulderblades and she crumpled to her knees. He had only to turn his wrist in her hair and, like a ball in a net, her head swung against the chest of drawers. He saw nothing, he knew nothing of the frenzy which possessed him. The human head lay lightly against his arm. Each blow he struck was more and more necessary, more and more strictly in proportion to his need to do the right thing, even to overdo it, to be passionately thorough in whatever he undertook . . . Blood spurted, surprising him, and he stopped short.

His hand held a tuft of hair, the body of a young woman lay at his feet, a dark stain spread on the carpet, the noise of the sea flowed back into his ears, surges of hot bile rose to his throat, he bent down to see who it was and recognized Blanche.

XXV

A large fly droned from wall to wall. It buzzed for a moment, plump and preoccupied, before falling silent. It was somewhere nearby, at rest on a piece of furniture. There were three of them now in this room with its windows wide to the universe. No star, no movement. The night sky beyond was drenched in the orange light reflected from the seawall; the air was thick with a smell of dung and algae; chairs and tables swam in a faint mist. He felt strangely well. Blanche slept. Tiny bubbles gurgled on the open wound, but her face was happy and at rest. He rose, switched off the ceiling light, and sat beside her. The fly went vigorously whizzing around once more. No music could restore like the buzz of this fly, to those who had lost them forever, the noons of childhood, the sunlit walls, the grassy space behind the church, the bread cupboard, the warm-tiled floor, the cows, the slow pendulum of their tails, the lizards, the blind happiness of those days . . . That these good thoughts, thanks to a little fly, should emerge from their obscurity and shine forth for them as if it were morning already! . . . He knelt beside Blanche on the carpet.

"We have a friend here," he whispered; "listen . . ."

In the same condition he always needed a little time to reply. He could have hung on her lips for hours, for nights on end, in this drowsy feminine odor, awaiting the birth of an exceptional word.

". . . can . . . hear . . ."

"You can hear it?" he exclaimed with delight. "It's a fly!"

So smooth was the skin of her averted face, so beautiful her halo of outspread hair, she seemed to have become again at last the woman he loved, hardly more than a baby in need of help to walk.

"Oh Blanche," he cried, "did you think I was going to lock you up in the house? I know how people get bored in houses! Just you wait," he said, crawling around her excitedly, "I've got other things in mind for us . . ."

". . . I . . . know . . ."

"Listen to me; I think . . . I *know* it, I *feel* it . . . I feel . . ."

His voice grew hoarse; tears fell from his cheeks onto Blanche's neck.

"Blanche, I feel . . . I feel that here . . . for us, here . . ."

". . . not . . . afraid . . ."

He supported her neck; he was sure she was smiling.

"Not afraid of what, Blanche? What are you not afraid of?"

And suddenly the same mad hope, the same trembling anticipation with which he had once awaited in the solitude of his room some unprecedented word, one word for himself alone, from the lips of the crucified Christ, a word of special guidance, fixed his gaze on this mouth already filled with the wings of a dark moth.

". . . dy . . . ing . . . ," she said.

Suddenly her fingers scratched at the carpet.

". . . hurts . . . hurts . . ."

He sprang to his feet in an instant crying:

"Off you go, then! Off you go, Blanche; I'm coming too! Go on, it's not much farther! Go on, look, there it is, there it is, we're there! . . ."

Kissing her mouth, stroking her breast, gasping in the depth of his throat, he squeezed her nostrils together. And Blanche, carried away by the whirl of noise and movement, the pain dissolving, shapes already dim, her tongue entwined with that of a stranger met in the street, in whom she had seen herself, abandoning all reserve as was her habit, abandoned life itself this Saturday night.

≈≈≈≈

To the memory of dead flies, squashed frogs, wasps burnt in their nests; to the memory of those birds who sang at night in times of insomnia, and that the fair-weather songsters might die for their vulgarity; to the memory of the murmur of great trees in the rain; to the memory of nettles bowing their pale heads over the graves of dead cats buried in biscuit tins; to the memory of Marie the grocery woman; to the memory of sly Anne-Clarisse; to the memory of Uncle Edward, worse than a bastard, a penitent; to the memory of matrimonial sheets drying in a country wind; to the memory of broken glasses, full ashtrays, and bandages found in the cold morning hearth of the drawing room; to the memory of moonlight through dormitory windows; to the memory of childhood medicine and pajama flights over wet earth; to the memory of sleep broken by sobs and prayers; to the memory of everything that, during this long, too long delay, was merely illusion and pale repetition until the revelation of the existence of an ideal girl, beautiful, generous, touching, willing to give anything, his head resting on Blanche's stomach, his pipe in his hand, alternately crying and laughing, he raised his glass.

XXVI

Before dawn on the third day, at the very hour Blanche had entered it for the first time, they left the room together and closed the door. Snuggling up to him, her cheek on his shoulder, drowsy behind her beautiful veil of hair, she looked sweet in a man's jacket that was too big for her. And the little skirt she'd worn the first evening, the little skirt she'd worn in Paris, what a sorry picture that little skirt presented! But to tell the truth, short or long, whatever this girl might wear and however tired she might be, she remained extraordinarily attractive.

Hip to hip, as in a three-legged race, they followed the corridor wall, pausing from time to time to lean against it. A harsh cough from behind a partition broke the silence, then a snore, and the sighs of somebody turning over in bed. They would all have breakfast delivered to them in a few hours: order forms hung from the doorknobs.

"Do you want me to carry you?" he whispered. "Take off your shoes . . ."

And, locked in each other's arms, leaving their shoes lined up at the door of room 412, they made their way to the elevator.

They emerged into the dark entrance hall and passed the reception desk, where two haggard, red-rimmed eyes, illuminated from below, appeared at counter level.

"Number 420," beamed Lucas without stopping. "We're going to be married."

"I hope you will be very happy," said the night porter.

Their voices echoed among the colonnades.

"*She* won't, I'm afraid," said Lucas; "you can see for yourself, monsieur."

"Champagne, I suppose . . ."

The roar of the sea filled the hall, then darkness engulfed them.

≈≈≈

The glow from the promenade picked out everywhere in furrows of light and shadow the footprints left on the beach, beyond which the ocean sang.

They staggered down to the foot of the steps. Through dips and ridges, tripping over each other, the two of them alone on the expanse of sand, they lurched away from the lights of the seawall. They proceeded slowly toward the horizon, one upright, the other stretched out in his arms, forming between them a single cross. Now one way, now the other, contentious winds impatiently combed their hair. Toes gripping the cold sand, eyes fixed on the line dividing sea from sky, he gained ground yard by yard. The ebb tide had opened the seabed; but the chambermaids of this world, to be difficult, were anxious to close it up and tuck it in. What was more agreeable, after all, than a wide-open bed? Moving flat-footedly in a straight line, he trod its wide expanse, while above him sheets of darkness rose and fell. Once in the shallows he quickly removed his clothes—an innocent precaution, since it was thus that he had come into the world. Blanche too, blanched white to her very hair, so that she shone.

His bride on his back, his great shirt tied like a loincloth at his waist, the arms he loved around his neck and his heart raging, he capered into the foam. It was cold, violent, festive; waves struck him twice without warning. He raised his head: let it not be said that in the water Lucas Boyenval failed to acquit himself like a man for as long and as far as his height permitted, on the two feet nature had given him . . . Chin up, a thigh under each arm like dripping fish it was his task to return to the sea, he advanced proudly to meet the waves to come . . . Presently it occurred to him that the waves were scared, huddling together in front of him before making a pitiful dash for the shore.

"Did you see that?" he laughed in their faces. "Just look at that one there!"

He saw sheep scrambling over one another at the approach of his motorbike, but the thought passed; for if the sea itself were going soft now, then truly the time had come to exchange worlds. And because the moon had laid a golden path for them; because the current was drawing them toward the open sea; because Blanche lay ever more gently, ever more lightly, on his back; because her soft lips continually kissed his shoulder, his ear, his shoulder, his ear; and because he was overwhelmed by a need to sleep, he closed his eyes and curled up in the cradle of the deep.

171 ≋≋≋